HIS
MIRACLE BRIDE

HIS
MIRACLE BRIDE

BY

MARION LENNOX

™ MILLS & BOON®

Pure reading pleasure

First published in Great Britain 2007
Large Print edition 2007
Harlequin Mills & Boon Limited,
Eton House, 18-24 Paradise Road,
Richmond, Surrey TW9 1SR

© Marion Lennox 2007

ISBN: 978 0 263 19509 5

Set in Times Roman 15¼ on 17 pt.
16-1207-55842

Printed and bound in Great Britain
by Antony Rowe Ltd, Chippenham, Wiltshire

PROLOGUE

BLAKE, Connor, Sam, Darcy, Dominic and Nikolai. And Pierce. Her self-contained sons.

Ruby looked along the long line of men and she sighed. She'd tried so hard, but they didn't get it. The gift in her purse—their combined gift for her seventieth birthday—spoke of failure more than anything else.

But her sons were wonderful, she thought, blinking back tears as she tried to see the happy side of the equation. Each one was making a difference in the world. What a transformation from the waifs she'd rescued from so many forms of neglect.

They were listening avidly to the speaker. So should she. The Earl of Loganaich was speaking at the opening of his refuge for disadvantaged children. As the past head of Foster Parents Australia, Ruby had been asked for advice. She'd been overjoyed at the concept. A place where kids could regroup...

Advice for Ruby was never enough. She'd talked her boys into contributing, with expertise as well as funds. They'd agreed without hesitation. Today they'd flown in from round the world, taking time out to share her pleasure. And using the occasion to give her their special birthday gift.

Ruby's birthday had been the week before. They hadn't forgotten, they'd told her, but they'd said they knew she hated family gatherings.

But it wasn't Ruby who hated family gatherings, she thought sadly. It was her boys. Her men. They saw emotion and they ran a mile.

The Castle at Dolphin Bay was a family enterprise. On stage now was the Earl of Loganaich and his Lady—Lord Hamish and Lady Susan. With them was their extended family: kids, friends, dogs, the whole domestic muddle. These people had come together to build something they believed in, and the joy of their shared enterprise—plus the joy of belonging to such a close-knit family—shone through.

The earl's speech was coming to a close. For the family on the stage it was hugs all round. Ruby looked sadly along her line of grown-up foster sons and there was none of that joy about them.

Today's gift had been as unexpected as it was unwanted—the deeds to a Sydney apartment overlooking one of the most glorious views in the world.

But… 'Anyone who wants to stay with you for more than a couple of weeks needs our consent,' her sons had told her. 'We're protecting you from yourself. It's time you stopped taking in the strays of the world.'

They didn't understand, she thought again sadly, an errant tear slipping down her wrinkled face. She'd fought so hard for all of them, and they'd succeeded, but they'd succeeded on their terms.

She sniffed, trying desperately to focus again on the owners and employees of this extraordinary castle. They seemed so happy. She just knew this place would be successful.

Would her boys ever be successful? On her terms? Successful in love?

Pierce had seen her tears. He was frowning, reaching across to take her hand. At thirty-six, Pierce was a brilliant architect, lean, craggy, and confident in his dealings with the world. But to Ruby Pierce would always be the starving, ill-used kid she'd rescued over and over again.

Pierce more than anyone had contributed to this day, designing the extensions to the castle buildings free of charge so it could more easily accommodate those it was designed to help. She knew Pierce had enjoyed the work, but still he held himself distant.

And where was this baby he'd told her about? The things he'd told her this morning had left her stunned. He'd been married but now his wife was dead? He was caring for a baby? She hadn't heard any of this until now, and it was only because she'd overheard Pierce talking to his foster brothers that he'd been forced to tell her.

'What is it, Ruby?' he asked her now.

'It's just… I'm so confused. I so wanted you to have a proper family.'

He gave a rueful smile. 'I do.'

It nearly killed him to admit even that much, Ruby thought. And family? Ha. 'One baby you're hiring a housekeeper to look after? You won't even let me near.'

'It's not as if this child's mine, and you've done enough. I can't let you.'

'But I want to.'

'No, you don't.' Pierce was a professional in charge of his world and she was a frail old lady who didn't know any better. Beloved but past her use-by date. 'You need to rest.'

'I've got all the time in the world to rest,' she whispered. 'But now…all I want is to live.'

She looked again along the line of her boys. Her outstanding men.

Not one of them knew how to live, she thought sadly. Not one.

She'd failed.

CHAPTER ONE

SHE'D psyched herself for farm terrors—but not for this.

Shanni steered her car onto the verge, but she didn't drive in the gate. No way.

Shanni wasn't a farm girl—in fact her best friend had burst out laughing when she'd divulged her destination. But Jules had grown up on a farm, so she'd talked Shanni through what she might face.

'Cows will ignore you as long as you don't interfere with their calves. Calves are curious but harmless, and most modern farms employ test tubes instead of bulls. Check if a cow has a dangly bit, and if it does don't go near it. Horses… Big doesn't mean scary. Say boo to a horse and it'll take itself off. Most farm dogs are all bluster. Look them in the eye and shout "sit." Oh, and watch for cow pats. They're murder on stilettos.'

So she'd left her stilettos at Jules's chic Sydney bedsit. She'd rehearsed her 'sit' command and she was ready for anything.

Anything but this.

There were kids sitting on the gate. Multiple kids. One, two, three, four.

They were watching her. Well, why wouldn't they? Shanni's car might well be the only car along here in a week. The meandering gravel track followed a creek that came straight from the snow melt. Distant mountains were capped with snow, even though spring was well under way. Undulating paddocks were dotted with vast red gums. The beauty of New South Wales's high country was world renowned.

But…

The cows looked safely enclosed in paddocks. She couldn't see a horse or a dog. What she saw was far more terrifying. Girl, boy, boy, girl, she decided, running down their ranks. Matching grubby jeans, T-shirts, sensible boots.

Siblings? Maybe, though there was a redhead, a blonde and two brunettes.

Forget the hair. They were sitting on the gate of the farm where she'd agreed to work.

She'd stuck her Aunty Ruby's letter on the dashboard so she could read the directions. Ignoring the kids—who were clearly waiting for her to do something—she reread it now, holding it like she was handling a scorpion.

Aunty Ruby's letter read like she talked—so fast she hardly paused for breath.

Pierce won't let me help him. He was always the sweetest boy. I'm sure you thought so, too, and he's had such a bad time. And now this. His wife died six months ago. His wife! He didn't even tell me he was getting married, that's how much he doesn't want to bother me, and now she's dead. And the boys are worrying about him. They say he's falling behind in his work. He's cutting corners, the boys say, and there's a huge contract he's risking losing. Mind, I think losing a wife makes any other loss irrelevant, but the boys won't talk about that. No one will. They treat me as if I'm ancient, not to be bothered.

Anyway dear, I know Michael broke your heart—at least your mother said he did though how you can love a man with a ponytail...but worse, you've lost your sweet little London gallery. If you were thinking about coming home... Could you bear to help with a baby for a few weeks until Pierce gets this contract sorted? He's been looking for a housekeeper but the boys say he's having trouble. I could go...but of course they won't let me.

Ruby's frustration sounded through the letter. Beloved Ruby, who'd spent her life helping others, was being held at arm's length by her foster sons, but she could no sooner resist sticking in her oar than she could breathe.

If she couldn't help, then she was sure that Shanni could.

And Shanni just might.

Housekeeper to a sort-of-cousin and his mother-less baby? On a farm on the other side of the world from her life in London? In the normal scheme of things, she'd laugh at the suggestion.

But this was Pierce MacLachlan…

Pierce was one of Ruby's many foster kids. At any family celebration, there'd always been three or four of Ruby's waifs.

There were three things affecting Shanni's decision to help him.

Number one was sympathy. She did remember Pierce. Twenty years ago, Pierce had been fifteen to her almost ten. She'd met him at her Uncle Eric's wedding and she'd been shocked. Ruby had just taken him in—'for the fourth time,' she'd told Shanni's mother. He'd looked far too skinny, far too tall for his clothes, far too…desolate.

And now he'd lost his wife. That was awful.

Shanni was a soft touch.

And, okay, admit it. Twenty years ago she'd thought Pierce had the makings of…gorgeous. Her hormones had just been waking up. Pierce was a tall, dark and mysterious fifteen-year-old, all angular bones and shadows. In truth he'd probably just been excruciatingly shy and malnourished, but he'd run rings round the rest of her rowdy cousins. So added to sympathy was…lust?

Yeah, right. She was a big girl now. Pierce was probably a five-feet-two midget with a pot belly. And she was supposed to be broken hearted.

But then there was number three, and that was the biggie. She didn't have enough money to stay in London. She'd lost her gallery and her lover. Ruby said Pierce had a farm. She could just pop in and see what the set-up was, and if it wasn't suitable then she could retreat to her parents' spare room and lick her wounds.

Only, the option of her parents' spare room was no longer available.

So she was here. Facing four kids.

Four kids? She was scared enough of one baby.

She couldn't stay, she thought, staring again at the four kids. But where to go? Where?

She hadn't done her homework before she'd headed home. She'd received Ruby's letter and suddenly she'd just come. To find that her parents were overseas—well, she'd known that—but to her horror they'd sublet their house. Hadn't they known their daughter was intending to need it? They might have guessed she'd flee to Australia without asking questions, to be met by strangers having a barbecue in their back yard.

She sniffed, but she didn't cry. When had she ever?

She should have cried when she'd found Mike in bed with one of his stupid models—but even then...

She'd come home mid-afternoon with the beginnings of the flu and had walked in and found them. Just like in the sitcoms, they hadn't seen her. Well, they'd hardly been looking.

She'd retreated to the laundry and filled a bucket. Then, while her whole body had shaken with suppressed rage—as well as the first symptoms of a truly horrid dose of influenza—she'd decided water alone wasn't enough. She'd stalked into the kitchen and hauled out the ice. Even then they hadn't heard her, though her hands were shaking so much she'd dropped two ice trays. It had taken five minutes before enough ice melted to bring the bucket of water to almost freezing, but it had definitely been worth the wait. Throwing it had been a definite high point.

Though, in retrospect, maybe tears would have been better. For, although she'd been ruthless with the ice bucket, she hadn't moved fast enough with the shared credit card. By the time she'd emerged from influenza and betrayal, Mike had revenged himself the only way a low-life creep with the morals of a sewer rat knew how.

It had been enough to tip her over the edge financially. Her tiny mortgaged-to-the-hilt art gallery had ceased to be.

But she was still irrationally pleased that Mike hadn't seen her cry. If I can cope with Mike without tears, I can cope with this, she told herself, staring out at the kids on the gate while her stomach plummeted as far as it could go and then found a few depths she hadn't known existed.

The kids were puzzled that she wasn't turning in. The oldest kid—a pre-adolescent girl with short, copper-red hair that looked like it had been hacked with hedge clippers—had jumped off the gate in preparation for opening it.

Surely she'd got it wrong.

She wound down the window—just a tad—admitting nothing.

'Is this Two Creek Farm?' she called.

'Yes,' the oldest boy called. 'Are you Shanni?'

'Yes.' Her voice was so faint it was barely a squeak.

'Finally.' The girl with the bad haircut hauled the gate wide while the three kids still sitting on the top rail swayed and clung. 'Dad says we can't go inside until you get here. What are you doing, parking over there?'

'Your dad's expecting me?'

'You rang. Didn't you?'

'Um… Yes.'

The girl looked right, looked left, looked right again—had there ever been another car up here?—and crossed the road to talk. 'Dad said, "Thank God, Ruby's come up trumps. We've got a babysitter."'

'I see.' She swallowed and looked again at the kids on the gate. 'I guess…your dad's name is Pierce?'

'He's Pierce MacLachlan.' The girl poked her hand in the open car window. She was all arms and legs and a mouthful of braces. 'I'm Wendy MacLachlan. I'm eleven.'

'I see,' Shanni said faintly, while her hand was firmly shaken.

'The others are Bryce and Donald and Abby,' Wendy told her. 'Bryce is nine. Donald's seven. Abby's four. There's Bessy as well, but she's only eight months old so she doesn't talk yet, and she's away with Dad. She's actually Elizabeth, but she's too cute to be an Elizabeth.'

Bessy. The baby. One true thing.

'Where's your dad?'

'He had to take Bessy to the doctor. We think she's got chicken pox. She hasn't got any spots yet, but she's grizzling so much she must be sick. Dad didn't get any sleep last night. When you rang he looked like he might cry.'

'Oh,' Shanni said. Even more faintly. She looked over to where the other three children were swinging on the opened gate. 'Have you all had chicken pox?'

'Oh yes,' Wendy said blithely. 'I had it first and then Donald and Abby and Bryce got it all together. Dad said he was going round the twist, but I helped.'

'I'm sure you did.'

'We didn't want Bessy to catch it, but she did anyway. Dad's buggered.' She blinked. 'Whoops, I'm not supposed to say that. Dad says. But when you rang and said you were coming Dad said, "Thank God, I'm so buggered I'll pay half my kingdom for decent help." And then he looked at all of us and said he'd pay all his kingdom.'

A lesser woman would turn around right now, Shanni thought. A lesser woman would say whoops, sorry, there's been a dreadful mistake, and go find a nice homeless shelter rather than face this.

'We shouldn't be here by ourselves,' Wendy admitted, her voice faltering just a little. 'But the station wagon's got a flat tyre, and when Dad pulled out the spare it was flat, too. Mum must have had a flat tyre and not told Dad… She swallowed. 'Before….before she died. Anyway, Dad's car's only a two-seater, and he really needed to take Bessy to the doctor and we won't all fit. So I said we'd be fine, only he worries about Abby cos she keeps doing stuff like getting her toe stuck in the sink. So I promised we'd sit on the gate and not move until you came. Abby promised faithfully not to fall off.'

'Ruby,' Shanni said to herself under her breath. Dear, dotty Aunty Ruby…

How could she cope with this? What she wanted was breathing space. Time to get her head clear, paint a little, take time to think about where she

wanted to go from here. A bit of wandering on a
farm, taking in the sights, maybe with a cute little
baby in a pram. Winning the gratitude of a boy she'd
once felt sorry for.

And solitude, solitude and more solitude.

There was a shriek from the other side of the road.
The boys had swung the gate hard and, despite her
promise, Abby had fallen backwards. The four-year-
old was hanging by the knees, her blonde pigtails
brushing the dirt. Her hands were dragging on the
ground, trying to find purchase, while the gate swung
wildly to and fro.

'Help,' she yelled. 'Wendy, *heeeelp*.'

Wendy sighed. She looked to the right, looked to
the left, looked to the right again and stomped back
across the road. The kid's boots look too tight, Shanni
thought. Her feet looked like they hurt.

Wendy yanked Abby backwards into her skinny
arms, staggering under her weight. The gate sung
wildly again with its load of two little boys.

'Are you coming in?' Wendy called across the
road, still staggering. Abby was far too heavy for her.

Shanni met her look head on.

It was a strange look for a child. She doesn't think
I'm coming in, Shanni thought. It was a look of a
child who'd needed to grow up before her time.
Despite herself, her heart lurched.

Oh, help. Stop it, she told herself. Stop it.

You're such a soft touch, her friends told her, and she knew they were right. Before she'd left London she'd had to find homes for the three cats she'd taken in against her better judgement, plus twenty cacti her elderly neighbour had persuaded her to water when she'd gone away for the weekend—only the weekend had turned out to be a decision to join her son in the Riviera for ever.

A lesser woman would have ditched the cacti. She hated cacti.

She'd boxed them up and taken them halfway across London to a batty cactus lover she'd found on the internet.

Even Mike… He hadn't had anywhere to stay, and he'd been such a promising artist. Had she mistaken sympathy for love?

So don't you dare feel sorry for this family, she told herself. Leave. Now.

But Wendy was watching her, her small face closed. She wasn't expecting help. And then she stopped looking at Shanni—decision made.

'It doesn't matter what Dad said,' she told her little sister. 'I'll take you inside.' She hugged her little sister in a gesture that was pure protection, turning her back on Shanni. 'You've scraped your fingers. We'll find a plaster.'

Oh, heck.

'What did you say your names were?' Shanni called.

'Bryce,' the oldest boy called. 'Bryce and Wendy and Donald and Abby. And Bessy at the doctor.'

'Okay, Bryce,' Shanni said wearily. 'Where do I park?'

'Definitely chicken pox,' the doctor told Pierce in a tone of deep disapproval. 'That makes the whole family. The older children should have been immunized. We do standard immunization at twelve months. Bessy will be paying the price of your failure to get that done.'

If he was less tired he'd slug him, Pierce thought wearily, but slugging would involve energy, and energy was something that was in short supply.

'Here's a prescription,' the doctor said, still cool. 'Twice a day, just like the older children. Can I rely on you to give it?'

'Yes,' Pierce snapped. Maybe he did have enough energy. But Bessy was clinging to his neck. It was pretty difficult to slug when holding a whimpering baby.

'The child welfare officer says you seem to be struggling,' the doctor said. He peered at Pierce as if he wasn't too sure. 'I can call them in, if you want. I told you that when their mother died.'

'I don't want. And I have help coming.'

'Excellent. I hope it's somebody competent. These children have suffered enough.' The doctor closed

Bessy's patient file with a snap. Consultation over. 'Let me know if you change your mind. I can get Welfare in tomorrow.'

The house was a tip.

Shanni walked into the kitchen and nearly walked out again.

It was a vast farmhouse kitchen, one wall almost taken up by a huge green Aga. The cupboards and benches were made of a deep, rich wood, and the floor was planked with something that looked like oak. An enormous wooden table dominated the room—a table big enough to…

To hold every eating utensil in the house, Shanni thought incredulously. When had they ever washed up?

'It's…it's a bit messy,' Wendy said, following Shanni in. She hadn't put Abby down. She was still staggering under her weight. 'Bessy was really sick yesterday.'

The two little boys were bringing up the rear. They at least looked like brothers—curly black hair, matching freckles, matching expressions of distrust.

The kitchen was cold. It was a glorious spring day but the place felt damp.

'We ran out of wood last night,' Wendy admitted, as she touched the cold stove. 'Dad ran out of time to chop it. But Dad said just as well, cos he wouldn't have gone to the doctor's and left the fire burning. We had cereal and orange juice for breakfast, so we didn't need the stove.'

'I see,' Shanni said. She didn't see.

Wendy staggered forward and plonked her little sister on a kitchen chair. 'I'll find a plaster.'

This at least was a place to start. Abby's finger was grazed. 'We need to clean it,' she told Wendy. 'Can you find me a face cloth and some soap?'

'I think so,' Wendy said cautiously. 'Are you going to look after us?'

'I have no idea,' Shanni told her. 'Or, not in the long term. But for now it looks like I need to look after you at least until your father gets home. Let's start with one sore finger.'

Bessy went to sleep somewhere between the doctor's surgery and the pharmacy. Finally. She'd sobbed practically all the previous night. She'd sobbed in the doctor's waiting room and in the surgery. The silence as she slid into sleep was almost deafening.

Pierce was lucky enough to find a parking space just outside the pharmacy. Yes! There was no way he was going to wake her.

But here was another occasion where he could be censured by child welfare—never leave your child alone in a car.

It wasn't like this was a closed-in car. His cute little sports coupé—a bright yellow MX5 he loved almost more than life itself—was open to the sun. It was a gorgeous spring day. He'd be able to watch Bessy though the window of the pharmacy as he dived in and grabbed the prescription.

But there were ten prescriptions before him.

'It'll be twenty minutes,' the pharmacist said, and Pierce almost groaned.

'I've got kids at home and the baby in the car.'

'Don't leave your child in the car.'

'Look, can you fast track…?'

'Twenty minutes.'

'Fine.' He sighed. He couldn't slug everyone in this town even if it was starting to feel like everyone was conspiring against him. 'I'll sit in the car and wait.'

He tried to stalk out, but his legs were too tired to stalk. As he walked past the window on the way out he caught a look at himself in its reflective glass.

He hadn't shaved for two days. He'd slept in these clothes.

He looked like death. A little old lady entering the pharmacy gave him a wide berth, and he didn't blame her.

He slid into the driver's seat of his cool little car. Beside him, Bessy was still soundly asleep.

'Twenty minutes, Bess,' he said, but she didn't stir.

He empathized. He sighed. He closed his eyes.

The warm spring sun was a balm all by itself. It was quiet. So quiet.

Twenty minutes.

He could just fold his arms on his steering wheel and let his head droop.

It was so warm….

'How long did you say your dad would be?'

'He said an hour. The appointment was for half past ten.'

'It's now well after eleven. Shouldn't he be back by now?' Shanni said cautiously.

'Yes,' Wendy said, and her bottom lip trembled. Just a bit. She caught herself almost before the telltale quiver happened, but Shanni had seen.

She felt like quivering herself.

Uh-oh.

She was only staying here until Pierce got home, she told herself. Then she was out of here fast. But these kids were starting to look more scared than she was. She couldn't leave them. Nor could she sit round in this appalling mess worrying about where Pierce was.

They were all staring at her, and Wendy's poorly disguised quiver was reflected on each of their faces.

They'd lost their mum. Pierce was late.

Their world wasn't as stable as they might like.

'Right,' she said. 'I'll ring the doctor's surgery, shall I?'

'Yes,' said Wendy, sounding relieved.

So she rang. Yes, he'd been at the doctor's surgery.

'He has to collect a prescription before he goes home,' the receptionist told her. 'And he's probably taken the opportunity to go shopping. Has he left those poor children by themselves?'

There was enough censure in her tone to make Shanni back off.

'No. They're with me.'

'If there's a problem…'

'Why would there be a problem?'

'The child welfare people aren't all that happy about the way he's coping.'

Her voice was loud enough for Wendy, clinging to Shanni's side, to hear.

'Tell her we're coping fine,' Wendy said, her face flushing. 'Yeah, Dad'll just be shopping. We're okay.'

'We're okay,' Shanni said, and put the phone down.

'They want to take us away from Dad,' Wendy said.

Maybe they, whoever they were, had grounds.

But meanwhile… She could hardly phone the police and report Pierce missing. Not yet. She'd give him a bit of leeway.

But there was still fear on four little faces.

'There's no earthly use looking like that,' she told them, mentally rolling up her sleeves, girding her

loins, doing whatever a girl had to do before launching into battle. 'If you're worried about child welfare,
then we need to show them we're coping.'

'How are we coping?' Wendy asked.

'By cleaning.' She stared at the mound of dishes.
'First thing first. This is a big job, so we need a major
battle plan. I'll chop enough wood to light the fire
and get some hot water. Lots of hot water. A sink
isn't going to cut it. Let's fill the bath. Donald, can
you find us a pile of clean towels? The rest of you
carry every dirty dish—except the knives, we'll leave
the knives for me—into the bathroom. Boys wash
and girls dry. I want the whole bathroom filled with
clean plates, so clean they sparkle. I'll clean in here,
and then we'll bring the clean things back in.'

'We can't,' Donald said. 'We're not old enough to
wash dishes. Only Wendy.'

'Nonsense,' Shanni said with a lot more briskness
than she felt. 'Big doesn't mean clever. Take your
boots and socks off so if you get wet it doesn't
matter. Washing in the bath is fun. Do you have a
sound system—for music?'

'P… Dad has one,' Wendy said. 'He's got lots of
CDs.'

'Then let's put on a bouncy work CD,' she said.
'Something like Abba. Do you know *Dancing Queen*?'

'Yes,' Abby said, her eyes lighting up. 'Our
Mummy liked Abba. That's why she called me Abby.'

'Then we'll put on Abba.'

'I don't know whether Dad's got Abba,' said Wendy.

Huh?

No matter. Questions could wait.

'Let's look then, shall we?' Shanni said, sounding a lot more decisive than she felt. 'Cos this house looks like it needs about a hundred Abba CDs to lick it into shape.'

At four o'clock the sun slipped behind the Craggyburn Post Office clock tower and Pierce and Bessy lost their sunshine.

Bessy woke first. She wiggled in her car seat, reached across to Pierce, put her pudgy hand into his mess of unkempt brown curls and pulled.

Pierce woke like he'd been shot.

'Mmmphf,' Bessy said in deep satisfaction at the results of one small tug.

'Bess,' Pierce said, coming to and trying to stop his eyes watering. 'Boy, you don't know your own strength.'

He winced and rubbed his head. He stirred and he stretched.

He gazed sleepily up to the clock tower.

The world stilled.

Surely he hadn't. Surely…

Oh, God, he had. He'd been away for over five hours. Almost six.

He reached for the ignition, his fingers fumbling in haste. A woman from the pharmacy was restocking shelves in the window. She saw him backing out of the parking space, and she waved to him frantically to stop.

He paused and she came to the door.

'Your prescription's filled,' she called. 'We wondered when you'd wake up. You should be more careful. Mr Connelly, the pharmacist, says the baby'll probably be sunburned.'

Not bad at all.

Shanni stood back and surveyed the pencil sketch she'd just done with a tinge of admiration. Her very first cow. It even looked like a cow.

Its leg looked a bit funny.

She checked her line of kids. Four kids. Four boards with paint, four brushes, four makeshift easels. Intense concentration. Good.

Four o'clock. How long before she called someone in?

She looked across at Wendy who was working with almost desperate absorption.

Donald, Bryce and Abby were silent, too.

Damn him. What was he playing at?

She should call…

Wendy looked across at her, her eyes pleading.

Not yet.

* * *

Pierce was struggling to stay under the speed limit as he and Bessy flew homeward. Bessy was rested and cheerful, crowing in delight at the soothing feeling of wind against her increasingly itchy skin.

Pierce might have rested but he didn't feel rested. He'd left them for an hour hoping the woman—who was it? Shannon? No, Shanni—would arrive.

Even if she had arrived, she'd be long gone by now. The kids would be terrified.

He turned the last curve—and there was a police car in the yard.

The police…

It'd be the pharmacist, he thought, remembering the prissy set to the man's mouth as he'd handed over Bessy's medicine. The whole town thought these kids would be better off in care. And now…

'I've stuffed it big time,' he told Bessy as he lifted her from the car. 'I don't deserve to have you guys.'

Where was everybody?

Two policemen appeared from behind the hayshed. Accompanied by a redhead.

A woman. Small. Slim. Faded jeans. Bright red windcheater, splodged with green paint. A yellow bandana catching back shoulder-length flaming curls. Green paint smeared on a snubbed nose. Freckles.

Memory stirred. One of Ruby's family weddings. A nightmare of being alone. A kid the same age as him, taunting, 'He's one of Aunty Ruby's strays. He's a bastard. Bastard, bastard, bastard.'

Then a skinny little girl, dressed in a scarlet party frock and with a huge pink bow in her flaming hair, marching up to her big cousin and stomping hard on his foot. So hard the kid had yelped.

'Gee, I'm sorry, Mac,' she'd said, and she hadn't sounded sorry at all. Then she'd turned to him and smiled. 'Hi. My name's Shanni. What's yours?'

He'd remembered. That tiny piece of kindness and bravado had stayed with him, to be used as an inward smile at need.

Could this really be her?

'Pierce, dear, we're over here,' she said, smiling brightly and waving to him like he was her long-time cousin. 'How's our darling Bessy? Did you get the things I wanted from the store?'

'Um…hi,' he said weakly, and the memory of the stomping was suddenly crystal clear.

Amazingly the cops were smiling as well. Pierce recognized them—an older cop who had family in the town, and a younger guy whose stock in trade was aggression. They'd been here two weeks ago with the child welfare officers.

They'd left then looking grim. They weren't looking grim now. The younger guy was smiling almost fatuously, and the older guy was looking on with benign amusement.

'So, Friday night…' the young cop said to Shanni.

'Can I let you know?' Shanni said. 'I need to sort out rosters with my cousin. It wouldn't do to leave the kids by themselves.'

Ouch.

'We'll see you round, then,' the older cop said benignly. 'Good luck with that cow, miss. I'm sure you'll get that leg right in the end.'

'I'll ring you on Friday,' the young cop said, waving a slip of paper. 'Thanks for your number. I won't lose it.'

They waved to Pierce in friendly salute. They climbed into the police car, and they were gone.

Leaving Pierce with Shanni.

CHAPTER TWO

'UM...YOU'RE Shanni,' he said, and he sounded dumb.

'You think?' Shanni said, arching her eyebrows. She'd stopped walking toward him the minute the police car left the yard. She didn't come one inch closer. 'You might want to check. After all, it's important to be sure who you leave in charge of your children.'

'Look, I...'

The bouncing smile and the charm were put carefully aside. 'What the hell are you playing at? Wendy's terrified. I came within an inch of telling those policemen that these kids would be better off in foster care. What sort of a father are you? *Where the hell have you been?*'

He focused on the one tiny thing he had control over. 'Do you mind watching your mouth? I'm teaching them not to swear.'

She took a deep breath. 'You are kidding?' she said at last. 'Abandoned, starving kids being taught not to swear.'

'They're not starving.'

'So what did you leave them for lunch?'

'I don't know,' he said, forcing his dazed brain to think. 'There's eggs, steak, sausages, frozen chips…'

'All of which require a stove,' she said dangerously.

'We've got a stove.'

'And the kids were going to light it how?' Shanni was looking at him like he was something that had crawled out of cheese.

'Look, I went to sleep.'

'Really?' She raised one quirky eyebrow. 'You had a little nap. So your kids starved.'

'Kids don't starve from missing lunch.'

She glared.

'Dad,' said a small voice, and it was Wendy, approaching from behind Shanni.

She stayed behind Shanni. She didn't come near. It was like she was using Shanni as a shield.

The weight around his heart grew heavier. He'd let Wendy down. This puny kid who had the weight of the world on her shoulders. He'd been gaining her trust. A little.

'Hell, Wendy…'

'Don't swear in front of the children,' Shanni said icily.

'Look, I fell asleep,' he said desperately. 'I didn't sleep at all last night. Wendy, tell her I didn't sleep. I had to take Bessy to the doctor's, and then I had to wait for the prescription to be filled. I sat in the car and waited because you can't leave kids alone in the car, and I just slept.' He spread his hands. He might never convince Shanni, he thought, but it was Wendy who was important.

There was a lengthy pause while Wendy considered. Shanni remained silent.

'He really didn't sleep last night,' Wendy said at last, talking to Shanni. 'Maybe he didn't sleep the night before, either,' she added. 'I had a nightmare and woke up. He made me hot chocolate.'

Shanni's iciness thawed, just a little. 'You're saying he has an excuse?'

'He looks awful,' Wendy said.

'He does,' Shanni agreed. 'When did he last shave?'

'He looks okay when he's shaved,' Wendy said. 'Or when he's a little bit bristly. He's too bristly now.'

This sisterhood thing was getting scary. But they were coming down on his side. Maybe.

'Oooohh.' It was Bessy, beaming at Wendy.

Wendy walked forward and snatched Bessy from his arms. Then she retreated behind Shanni again. They weren't completely on his side. Wendy must have been terrified.

'I'm really sorry,' he told her, while Shanni practised her glare some more.

'I thought you'd run away,' Wendy said.

'I won't. I told you.'

'Men tell lies. Mum said that. Men always tell lies.'

There was another lengthy pause, worse than the last. Pierce tried to think of what to say. Nothing came.

The silence extended. The three of them were gazing at him like he was a maw worm. Wendy and Shanni…even Bessy.

Then, 'You know, my dad doesn't tell lies,' Shanni said, thoughtful. 'Honest. And I've known my dad for twenty-nine years. He makes mistakes—once he even left me at the ice rink for five hours cos he was reading a really good book—but he doesn't tell lies. Are you hungry?' she asked him.

Food was the last thing he was thinking of. *Though, come to think of it…*

'I guess I am a bit.'

'There's cold sausages,' Wendy said. 'We cooked a lot for lunch cos we thought you'd be home. And Shanni made choc-chip cookies.'

'Shanni's made choc-chip cookies?' He stopped looking at Wendy. Yep, he'd betrayed a trust, and somehow he had to figure out a way to retrieve himself—but there was nothing he could do about that right now. But somehow Shanni's ice-rink story had lessened the tension. And sausages… Choc-chip cookies…

'They're my specialty,' Shanni said modestly. 'You didn't have choc chips so we had to squash a block.'

'The fire's not lit.'

'We lit it,' Wendy said. 'We had to light it to get

hot water to do the dishes. And I've eaten five choc-chip cookies.'

'You lit the fire? But the wood...'

'Shanni chopped it. The boys stacked it. The wood box is full.'

Shanni had chopped the wood. She'd lit the stove. She'd made choc-chip cookies. He stared.

'I know,' she said, pseudo-modest. 'Call me Wonderwoman.'

'Ruby said you're an artist.' His tone was almost accusatory. He heard it, and tried desperately to retrieve himself. 'I mean...'

'I think I'm converting to wood chopping,' Shanni said. 'I've failed cows' legs, and chopping vents anger.'

'Anger...'

'Now, why would I be feeling anger?' she said, to Wendy rather than him. 'To be brought here under false pretences...'

Whoa. Things were spinning away from him. 'False pretences?' he said weakly.

'One baby,' she said, and tugged Wendy against her in another display of the power of sisterhood. *Men,* the gesture said. The despicable species. 'One baby does not equate to five kids. Ruby told me one baby. I rang you from my friend's and you said one baby.'

Uh-oh.

'I didn't say one baby,' he said weakly. 'But, yeah, Ruby would have told you one baby. To be honest, when you rang I thought I'd get you here any way I could and try and bribe you into staying once you got here.'

Beam me up now, Scotty, he thought bleakly. I'm an outright bastard.

But suddenly they had a diversion. Bessy had been nestling against Wendy's shoulder, content from her drive. But Bessy was eight months old. She hadn't been fed since breakfast. She was a young lady with chicken pox.

Bessy suddenly recalled all this in one huge momentous wash of outrage. She opened her mouth, and she yelled.

'Can you stay at least until we've fed Bessy?' Pierce asked over the yells.

'I'm staying until you've done some explaining,' Shanni said grimly. 'I need to murder you or I need to murder my Aunty Ruby, and I can't figure out which.'

She should leave.

Since Bessy's initial howl there'd been no time to do anything but run. There certainly hadn't been time for explanations.

Bessy had needed feeding, bathing, soothing, more soothing, more feeding. The kids had needed baths and dinner. The cattle had needed feeding. Okay, Pierce had done that one on his own. Shanni had stayed in the kitchen and supervised the kids' dinner while watching Pierce out the window.

There was a huge cow—a bull?—in the paddock closest to the house. Pierce had wheeled a vast bale of hay to the gate on a hand cart, opened the gate and spread the hay.

Wasn't that dangerous? The cow had looked... looked...

Cute, she'd decided as Pierce had scratched it behind the ear. The big creature had almost purred, leaning its big body against Pierce until he staggered. Really cute.

Actually, not as cute as Pierce.

He was tall and lean and angular. His deep brown curls were unkempt and too long. He hadn't shaved for a couple of days and he had shadows under his eyes. His jeans and windcheater looked like he'd been sleeping in them. He looked almost gaunt.

Her impression of Pierce aged fifteen had been that the guy was hot.

Nothing had changed.

What wasn't hot was five children.

But she did feel sorry for him. To be stuck with five kids...

It was his choice.

It was hardly his fault that his wife had died.

No, but...

'What are you thinking?' Wendy asked shyly. The

kids were tucking into scrambled eggs like there was no tomorrow.

'I'm thinking you guys have hollow legs. What have you been eating?'

'Pie… Dad's not a very good cook.'

'Do you call him Pierce?'

'Yes, but not in front of people,' Bryce told her, scooping up another mouthful of scrambled egg and closing his eyes in bliss. 'This hasn't got a single bit of black on it.'

'Scrambled eggs is my second specialty, after choc-chip cookies.'

'Pizza's Dad's specialty,' Wendy said. 'But the last time we ordered it Dad forgot we didn't have any cash and the pizza guy wouldn't take a cheque or credit card and now he won't come back.'

'I can make pizza.'

'You're kidding.' It was Pierce, standing in the doorway, surveying the domesticity before him with amazement. 'You cook pizza?'

'She means she gets those boxes in the supermarket and thaws them out,' Bryce said wisely.

'I do not,' she said, taking umbrage. 'I can cook them from the ground up.'

'Will you cook us one?' Abby asked.

'Maybe tomorrow. If I get the ingredients.'

'Will you stay then?' Donald was the quietest of the kids. He'd hardly spoken since she'd arrived.

He'd simply watched her. Even when she'd set them all to painting, she'd been aware that Donald had never stopped watching her. Now he asked his question and it was like a challenge.

'For tonight.' She blinked. Yeah, okay, she was committing herself, but where else was she going to sleep? 'Tell me you have a spare bed.'

'We have a spare bedroom,' Pierce said.

'It's Mummy's bedroom,' Donald said, still gazing at her with that unwavering stare.

Mummy's bedroom. Oh, heck. 'Um, doesn't Daddy sleep there?'

'He sleeps upstairs in Bessy's room,' Abby said.

'She keeps waking up,' Bryce added.

'Wendy used to get up to her when Mummy was sick,' Donald said, tilting his chin. 'Cos Mummy didn't want Pierce to. But Pierce does it now.'

'Didn't your mummy die when Bessy was born?'

'Just after,' Donald said.

This was stuff she didn't understand. She wasn't sure that she wanted to try. 'Isn't it bedtime?' she asked weakly, and Pierce nodded.

'It surely is.'

'Will Shanni tell us a bedtime story?' Abby asked.

'I will,' Pierce said gruffly.

'We want Shanni,' Wendy said.

'I'm washing up.' Shanni was feeling completely confused. What was going on here? Pierce looked defeated. Battle weary and exhausted. And he'd slept today.

'Your dad reads you bedtime stories,' she managed. 'That's his job. I'm the housekeeper—I keep house. It's up to Pierce to keep kids.'

Pierce took almost an hour to read them their stories. When he finally came downstairs, Shanni was sitting on the kitchen floor surrounded by stuff.

The more he looked at her, the more he remembered that ten-year-old Shanni. She'd made him smile then and she had that power still, just by sitting in the middle of his kitchen floor. Which was dumb. Dangerous, even.

'What you doing?' he managed.

'This isn't a fridge, it's an ecosystem.' She carefully didn't look at him. Instead she held up a jar where purple fuzz fought with green slime. 'Didn't Fleming invent penicillin this way? Are you searching for a patent cure for chicken pox?'

'Leave it.'

'Hand me a rubbish bag,' she said. 'Left to breed, this could take over the world.

He found a rubbish bag and held it out. She scooped in so much stuff that even he was hornswoggled.

'I'm usually neat,' he said defensively, and she nodded.

'I remember you at fifteen. You were…neat.'

He glowered. 'I believe I was wearing a suit.'

'Blue pinstripe if I recall.'

'That the rest of the boys thought was…'

'Poncy. Yeah, I remember you were teased.'

He gazed down, trying to figure things out. Where did she fit? He couldn't remember. Ruby had simply referred to her as 'our Shanni'. *Our Shanni would love to come and help out.*

All he could remember was the oversized bow and the stomping foot and the smile. Mostly the smile.

'I can't exactly remember the connection,' he said apologetically.

'My dad is Ruby's younger brother.'

'So you are…?'

'Lucy and Will's daughter. They're academics. They're currently in Switzerland.'

'I don't remember Lucy and Will. But I remember you.'

'Gee, thanks.'

'You stood on Mac's toe.'

'I did, didn't I?' she said, and grinned at the memory. 'He's grown up to be a used-car dealer. Ruby says he married a woman who's a real harpy. Good old Mac.'

'Why did you come?'

'Aunty Ruby asked me.' She held up something greenish. 'Courgette?'

'Cucumber.'

'A bit past its use-by date, wouldn't you say?'

'I— Yes.'

'Why didn't you tell me you had five kids?'

'I don't believe I told you anything.'

'But Ruby didn't say.'

'Ruby doesn't know.'

'Ruby doesn't know you have five kids?'

'No.'

'You didn't tell Ruby?'

'I barely see Ruby. There's no need to tell her everything.'

'Yeah, so omit a little something. Like four kids. Something's rotten here and I don't know what.' She'd been foraging in the rear of the fridge and now she emerged triumphant. 'No, this is dried out. I'm sure it's a courgette.'

'Could we cut this out?'

'Cleaning?'

'The inquisition.' He raked his fingers through his hair. 'And will you get off my floor? I hardly know you.'

'You know me enough to trust me with your kids.'

'I had no choice. I had a doctor's appointment and there was no other available appointment until tomorrow. I loaded the kids in the car, then realized the tyre was flat and so was the spare. You were coming. Ruby said you were trustworthy. So I trusted.'

'You left me alone deliberately?'

'No,' he roared, so loudly that there was a whimper from above their heads.

'You've woken Bessy,' Shanni said.

'Shush.'

They both shushed. Bessy whimpered again, and then settled.

'Take that outside,' Shanni said, motioning to the rubbish. 'It's disgusting.'

He did. It gave him room to take a few deep breaths. He stared up at the night sky and counted to ten. Then he decided to count to a hundred.

Finally he figured he'd better return. Shanni was still cleaning his fridge. All he could see of Shanni was one very cute, denim-clad butt emerging from his refrigerator.

He took a couple of moments to admire the view. Hell, he missed women. Twelve months now of enforced celibacy. Twelve months down and how many to go?

Not months. Years. What had he let himself in for?

'You want a whisky?' he asked the butt, and the butt stilled.

'A whisky?'

'Don't say it like I'm the local lush,' he said. 'I allow myself one whisky when all the kids are in bed. Surely a man can have that without being accused of child neglect?'

'Hey, I didn't say…' She was backing out of the refrigerator, butt wiggling.

'You didn't have to say. You were implying.'

'Actually I wasn't,' she said, sitting up and wiping a strand of wilting lettuce from her nose. 'I wasn't implying anything. I was about to say that a whisky would be very nice indeed. And if it turns into two then I'm not going to report anyone to Social Welfare. Just so long as I can share.'

She smiled.

He stared. It was the cutest smile. Wide and white and cheerful, green eyes dancing behind it.

Hey, cut it out. This was not appropriate.

Hell, he'd lost sense of what was appropriate or not. He ran his fingers through his hair again—yeah, he'd meant to get a haircut but when was there ever time? Then he decided he was staring at her and wondering about haircuts when he should be pouring whisky.

He turned on his heel and headed for the living room. He poured two decent tumblers, decided ice was for sissies and headed back to the kitchen.

She was still on the floor.

'You want to sit at the table?'

'If I get up I might never get down again.'

'The fridge can wait. You've done so much cleaning I'm feeling like a—' He hesitated. He didn't know what he felt like, he thought. Out of control? Yeah, maybe even more out of control than when his house had been full of dirty dishes.

'You must really miss your wife.'

He'd reached down to give her a hand up. He

stilled and Shanni stared at his hand, shrugged and heaved herself up. He shook himself.

'Sorry.'

'Hey, don't apologize. I only lost my boyfriend and I'm doing dumb things, like not contacting my parents and making sure they hadn't changed the locks before I come all the way to Australia.'

'They've changed the locks?'

'And put in tenants,' she said grimly. 'You'd think a daughter would know.'

'You're not close?'

'See, there's the thing,' she said, sitting at the table and taking her first sip of whisky. She wrinkled her nose in appreciation. 'I thought we were. I phone once a week. You'd think changing locks would be something they'd mention.'

'I… I guess.'

'Sorry.' She took another sip. 'We were talking about you. Your wife.'

'You lost your boyfriend?'

'He didn't die,' she said darkly. 'More's the pity.'

'Right,' he said, distracted. She looked really cute when she talked darkly. 'So you just lost him?'

'He went to bed with a model.' She glowered some more. 'In my bed. And then when I threw ice water over the pair of them he went out and spent our shared credit card to the hilt, and he isn't even sorry.'

She glowered at the absent boyfriend and model.

'But we're talking about you. You and the five kids and the dead wife and Social Welfare. I've never seen such a mess.'

'Thank you.'

She blinked. Then she put the whisky very carefully on the table.

'I'm sorry,' she said. 'I've had a long day. I landed in Sydney at five this morning. I took a cab to my parents' and found they'd absquatulated. So I took my dad's car and drove to my girlfriend's apartment, to find a bedsit smaller than a shoebox. Then I remembered Ruby's letter and rang you and asked if you still wanted a housekeeper, and you said yes, it'd be fine if I came straight away, so I ended up here. To find you'd absquatulated as well.'

'Absquatulated?' he said, distracted.

'Taken yourself off to points unknown, generally leaving a mess behind. My mother's a linguistics professor. Get over it.'

'Right,' he said, feeling dazed. 'I didn't... absquatulate.'

'You just went to sleep.'

'I've said I'm sorry.'

'The kids were terrified. They were thinking they'd get carted off to care.' She wrinkled her nose some more, perplexed. 'See, that's the part I don't get. Why is Welfare so interested in you? Have you done something awful? I mean, today was appalling, but that sort of mess happens in the best families. If I told you how many times my parents forgot me… Anyway, that's beside the point. I understand your wife dying was awful but Social Welfare isn't usually a monster.' She paused, thinking things through.

'You know, unless things are really dire, the authorities don't take kids from parents. I can't see them dragging children off to foster care just cos their dad went to sleep in the sun after a night with a sick baby.'

'No. I…'

'So have you done something ghastly? I mean, not that you'd confess. But I've been scrubbing the fridge and thinking that I should just leave. Except that I'm broke and I don't have anywhere to go. Except Aunt Ruby's.'

'You don't want to go to Ruby's?' He was having trouble keeping up.

'Ruby has macramé meetings in her kitchen every weekday morning. She's offered to teach me. And she says she has to get your permission anyway if she wants to have me for more than just a couple of weeks. Which is weird.' She hesitated. 'But you're sidetracking me. I keep thinking of Wendy. Wendy like she was when I arrived. Terrified. Expecting the worst. There must be something horribly wrong for her to look like that. I don't know what it is, and maybe I should leave, but I've decided I need to figure it out. Because now I'm hooked. If you're hurting these kids I'll—'

'You'll what?'

'I don't know,' she confessed. 'I can't figure out why they're terrified. Because the way you cuddle Bessy... You even seem nice.'

'Thank you.'

'You know what I mean. You look normal.'

'Yet I was a fifteen-year-old in a pinstripe suit when first you met me.'

'You're distracting me.' She looked at his whisky glass. He looked at it too.

'You do think I'm a drinker.'

'Hey, I just wondered. I mean, if I had five kids and a dead wife I might crack as well. And it would explain.'

'It explains nothing.'

'Then you need to give me some other explanation,' she said. 'Because I want to know why your kids are terrified.'

He stared into his whisky glass.

'Tell me or I retreat to macramé.'

His eyes flew to hers. He expected to see laughter, but he didn't. She was deadly serious.

She really cared, he thought. She was worried about these kids.

The sensation was so novel that he blinked.

'There's a simple explanation,' he said, meeting her look head on.

'Which is?'

'These aren't my kids. They're nothing to do with me. Until twelve months ago I'd never seen any of them before in my life.'

CHAPTER THREE

THERE was a long pause. Shanni had pulled open the fire door of the oven, to let the warmth of the flames give comfort to a kitchen that was only just warming up. The fire crackled behind them. He should put music on or something, he thought inconsequentially. The atmosphere was too intimate.

Maybe music would make it worse.

'They're not your kids,' she said at last. She wasn't taking her eyes off him, seemingly ready to judge by how he looked as well as what he said.

'No,' he said. There was nothing else to say.

'I did wonder,' she said mildly. 'They don't look like you. They keep forgetting to call you "Dad". And they didn't know if you had Abba.'

'Abba?'

'Never mind. I thought maybe they'd been calling you "Pierce" and you'd made them change for the welfare people.'

'I made them change for the welfare people.'

'But…' She sighed. She downed the dregs of her

whisky, looked at the bottle and sighed again. 'I've got jet lag and a muddled head,' she confessed. 'Don't give me any more whisky.'

'And Bessy's likely to be up in the night.' He rose and took the whisky bottle into the next room, returned and closed the door firmly behind him. They both looked at the door with longing. But no. They were mature adults, and there were no answers in a whisky bottle.

'I'll make coffee,' he said and she nodded. Mature adults. Coffee. Right.

'You'd better tell me,' she said, while he fiddled with cups and kettle and instant coffee. Instant. She'd come from the coffee centre of the world. *Agh.*

'I married their mother,' he said.

'Right.' She thought about it. 'So Bessy's yours?'

'No.'

'So Bessy's not yours.'

'They're none of them mine.'

'So when did you marry their mother?'

'Seven months ago. Just after Bessy was born. Three weeks before Maureen died.'

'Oh,' she said in a small voice. 'I see.'

'Do you?' He sounded angry. He had his back to her but she could hear tension and anger—and resentment.

'Hey, I cleaned your fridge,' she said. 'I'm the patsy in this set-up.'

Anger faded. His shoulders shook—just a little. 'The patsy?'

'The pig in the middle. The girl with the soggy cucumber. Shoot around me, but not at me.'

'I'm sorry.'

'That's better,' she said approvingly as he carried mugs of coffee across to the table. He really was good looking, she thought absently. And that hair was so ruffled. She could just reach over and touch it…

Cut it out, she told herself fiercely. What is it with you and long-haired men?

'Tell me about Maureen,' she said instead and took a mouthful of coffee, swallowing regrets about a magnificent coffee maker she'd left behind in London. Okay, it was Michael's, but it had been bought with her credit card and it made the best coffee. And that rat…

She wasn't thinking clearly.

'Maureen,' she said again, and Pierce looked confused.

'Look, I'm jet lagged,' she said. 'I'm not making sense to me.'

'You suddenly looked a long way away.'

'I was mourning coffee. Tell me about Maureen.'

'She was my foster sister sort of.'

There was a pause. Sort of foster sister. Hmm.

'Ruby only fosters boys.'

'You think I'm telling lies?'

'I'm not thinking anything,' she said. 'Thinking hurts.'

'She's great, your aunt Ruby.'

'She's lovely to everyone.'

'I guess.'

Whoops. 'I'm sorry,' Shanni said repentantly. 'I dare say you and Ruby have a lovely, personalized, meaningful relationship and I wouldn't dream of disparaging it.'

He choked on his coffee.

'She's a bit…batty,' he said, and Shanni grinned.

'We're together on that one. But you'd better tell me the rest.'

'It's not much use.'

'You want me to finish the refrigerator?'

'I…'

'Okay, I'll finish the refrigerator anyway,' she said, and gave him a rueful smile. 'I'm a sucker for a job well done. But tell me or I'll bust.' She pulled up a spare kitchen chair, put her feet up, had a couple of sips of coffee—*ugh*—and forced herself to relax. 'You're one of Ruby's strays. That must have been hard.'

'I guess.' He shook his head. 'No. I had a mother who didn't want me but wouldn't put me up for adoption. The times with Ruby were not the hard times. You come from a nice normal family.'

'Are you kidding?'

'Well, a family with a mum and a dad, and I'd imagine you were wanted.'

She thought of her eccentric parents and she grinned. 'Yep. They wanted me. They weren't quite sure what to do with me when they got me—they still aren't—but they wanted me.'

'I was a mistake.'

She looked at his stern face. There was a curl dripping over his left eye. She could just…

Cut it out!

'You were a mistake?

'My mother got pregnant during an affair with a very wealthy man. She thought getting pregnant would force him to marry her. She was wrong.'

'Oh.'

'And he denied everything. I can imagine my mother might have been a bit…' He sighed. 'Anyway, there wasn't DNA testing back then. She was screwed. So she put me into foster care, but every time she started a relationship she pulled me out again. To play happy families. And one of those relationships included Maureen.'

'I don't understand.'

'No, well…' He shrugged. 'You have no idea what drop kicks my mother used to fall for. Jack was maybe the worst. But he had a kid, too. Maureen. He ended up abandoning her, but when he met my mother Maureen was nine and I was seven.'

'So?' Shanni prodded. He looked like he was a long way away—remembering. He was staring straight through her. Now he gave himself a slight shake, as if tugging himself back to now.

'Okay. Dreary story. Jack was a sadist, but my mother thought everything he did was wonderful. So we were at his mercy. But Maureen was older and a bit harder than me. And for some reason she decided she liked me.' He shrugged. 'Okay, let's be honest. I loved the idea of having a big sister, and she thought having a brother was cool. It wasn't like we had anything else.'

The words chilled her and she winced, but Pierce didn't notice. He was seeing back, a long time ago.

'She was there for me,' he said softly. 'It was the longest of any of my mother's relationships. We were together two years. And every time he…' Once more a shrug. 'Well, she was always there for me. She'd fly at Jack like a tigress, biting, scratching, yelling. She'd end up as badly beaten as me but it got so… Well, he knew when he raised a hand to me he had us both to contend with, and it helped.'

'Oh, hooray for Maureen,' Shanni said shakily, and Pierce nodded, faintly smiling.

'She was great.'

'And then?'

'Then my mother and Jack split, and we were put in different foster homes. We tried to stay in touch,' he said sadly. 'Maureen used to write. Every six months or so I'd get a scrawly letter telling me what she was doing in her life. Then when we reached adulthood the letters ceased. The last letter said she'd met the man of her dreams and was moving to Perth.'

'But he wasn't? The man of her dreams?'

'Who'd know?' Pierce said bitterly. 'All I do know is that Maureen was wild as be damned. From what I've learned since, she seemed bent on self-destruction.'

'Drugs?' Shanni thought of the five children. 'No...'

'She didn't do drugs. That would have been suicide. She was diabetic.'

'Oh.'

'She just wanted kids,' Pierce said wearily. 'All her life she wanted a family—maybe that was why she was so defensive of me—and she was going to get a family no matter how much it took.'

'But the diabetes...'

'That's what I meant about self-destruction. Every time she got pregnant her body seemed to disintegrate. Only she just couldn't seem to stop herself.' He hesitated. 'She'd meet some lowlife and think he was the answer to her prayers and end up pregnant.'

'But not with you?'

'She'd been in Western Australia,' he said. 'We'd lost touch completely. Only then, just under a year ago, she came to find me. I was doing very nicely as an architect in Sydney. I'd bought this place as a weekender. I'm a confirmed bachelor, and I was pretty content with what life was dealing me.'

'But?'

'But Maureen's kidneys were failing. She was pregnant and refusing to terminate, but she'd been told the pregnancy would destroy what was left of her kidneys. She sat in my office in Sydney and she told me everything about her life. She spelled it all out, and she asked for my help. She hated asking, but she was desperate.'

'Oh Pierce.'

'Maureen was so ill she was facing having to have the children fostered. She couldn't bear subjecting them to the life she'd had. She'd brought it on herself but, well, maybe I could see what was driving her. And, while she was talking, that time…the times she took the beating for me came back. I didn't have a choice. There's a dialysis unit at Murribah, half an hour north of here. I offered her a home here for as long as she needed.'

Silence. She stared across the table at him for a long, long moment. Then she smiled. 'I always thought you were a nice boy,' she said warmly. 'Despite the pinstripes.'

He smiled back, but it cost him a bit, that smile. It was hard for him to tell this story, she thought.

'Okay. Moving on. You asked for the whole story so you'll get it. I was already having trouble with the neighbours here. What I didn't realize when I bought this place was that one of the bidders was a huge dairy corporation. They'd been looking for a site for their new factory, which would have meant the locals didn't have to pay cartage for their milk. But I'd fallen in love with the place and paid more than it was worth. So the factory went somewhere else. Then I'd no sooner taken possession when along came four kids and a mother who looked desperately sick and was pregnant again. I drove a bright yellow sports car when the kids looked starving. Maureen wouldn't talk to anyone about her background, and no one ever asked me. I've been judged and found wanting in just about every respect.'

She swallowed. 'I'm so sorry.'

'Don't be. I'm sorry enough for myself. Anyway, Maureen had Bessy and she grew even more ill. We were hoping against hope for a transplant but it didn't happen.'

'So…marriage?'

'You see, Social Welfare had taken care of these kids before, in periods when Maureen was desperately sick. So the kids were on file. It's not hard to understand. There are good people in the department who were genuinely worried. Then we had the community bad-mouthing us. Maureen started believing—and maybe she was right—that as soon as she died they'd send the kids to foster homes, regardless of what I wanted.'

'There are some good—' she started cautiously, but he was before her.

'You don't need to tell me there are some great foster homes,' Pierce said explosively. 'Foster parents are some of the best people in the world. Generous, big hearted, taking on all comers even though getting attached comes at the price of having their hearts ripped out over and over.'

'Goodness,' she said. 'Did I hit a nerve?'

He managed an apology for a smile. 'Yes,' he said, consciously lowering his voice. 'Sorry. If I hadn't had Ruby I'd be in such a mess now. But I was on my own, and these kids aren't. Despite Maureen's often incompetent care, they love each other, and they'll defend each other to the death. They should never be separated, and there's the problem. You think there'll be a foster parent who'll take on five kids?'

'I guess… Maybe not.'

'They'd be put into a group home,' he said. 'The welfare people told Maureen that, as if it was something good. A house in the community with paid carers. That's what Maureen couldn't come to terms with. A series of people employed to care. Maureen hated the idea, and by the time she became desperately sick I hated the idea as well. You've seen Wendy. She's been Maureen's principal carer for years. It took so long to teach her that I could help. Even now she doesn't completely trust me. Why should she? But I couldn't bear… I just couldn't bear…'

'So you married their mother.'

'Yes. We moved fast, in the window of opportunity before Maureen became too ill. We married. I applied to legally adopt them. Maureen filed everything saying she approved, and she assigned me as their legal guardian.'

'Oh, Pierce.'

'It's not noble,' he said. 'At least, it wasn't supposed to be noble. I'm paid ridiculous amounts for the work I do. I thought I'd house the kids, employ a housekeeper, someone to run the farm and come down here on weekends.'

'But?'

'Have you any idea how hard it is to find a housekeeper for five kids? In this community? I found a woman who did intermittent babysitting for a while, but the kids hated her and she quit two weeks ago. And now we've had chicken pox followed by school holidays. I'm going round the twist.'

'I see that you are.'

'And then Ruby said she'd contacted you and persuaded you to give us a try. Hence I've had one day of child care, a clean kitchen and a sparky clean fridge. And kids who weren't taken away from me today. For which I'm eternally grateful.' He hesitated. 'Shanni, dare I ask that you'll stay?'

'I'm not a housekeeper.'

'You're excellent at scrubbing.'

'That's only because I'm suffering severe loss of pride. I need to vent my spleen. Scrubbing works.'

'Ruby says you're an artist.'

'I'm not.'

'No?'

'I love dabbling with paints. Did you see my cow this afternoon? Perfect, except for one leg looking longer than the others. I measured it. It's not. It's perspective, but I can't work it out.'

'So you're an abstract artist?'

'I did a degree in fine arts. I worked as a curator for a tiny gallery here and an even tinier one in London. Then I scraped up enough money to open my own. It was miniscule, but it was devoted to one particular kind of art that I love. My parents lent me money. I didn't eat. I put everything into it that I had.'

'And?'

'And like I said, I caught my artist boyfriend in bed with one of my models. I tossed ice water on them, and he retaliated by using my credit card to spend a fortune. I had the choice of risking my parents' money and keeping on trying or bailing out. I bailed out.'

'Ouch.' He hesitated. 'You never tried recovering your money?'

'He said he'd have me for assault.'

'I see,' he said cautiously. 'So you fled home.'

'Yep. To you.'

'And now?'

'I'll go to Ruby's. I'll get a job somewhere and move on.'

'But it'd help if you could stay here for a bit while you regroup?'

'It might,' she admitted. 'But I don't intend to fall in love with these kids.'

'Of course not.'

'So don't even think I might be a long-term proposition.'

'I'm not looking for a long-term proposition.'

'I don't fall for kids. I don't fall for you.'

Uh-oh. Why had she said that? It had come from nowhere but suddenly it was important that she say it.

He so needed a shave. He looked so vulnerable.

Stop it. She gave herself a sharp metaphoric slap to the side of the head. *Do not fall for Pierce MacLachlan because you feel sorry for him.*

'Just because I'm a soft touch...' she whispered, and he smiled.

'Two of us. Two soft touches. We're doomed.'

'Speak for yourself.'

There was another whimper from above his head, but this time it didn't stop. It built fast to a wail. He winced, set his coffee mug down with a sigh and rose. 'She slept for three hours. I can't expect much more.'

'What will you do now?'

'Cuddle her until she goes back to sleep.'

'Ruby said you're not getting work done.'

The yells from upstairs were getting more insistent. 'Define "work". But I guess it doesn't matter. I just take one day—one moment—at a time.' He walked to the door and then paused. 'Shanni, you've helped me enormously today and I'm deeply grateful. If you leave right now I'll still be grateful. I won't put any more pressure on you. But you do need a bed for at least tonight?'

'Wendy showed me her mother's bedroom. She'd already made up the bed.'

'Wendy wants you to stay.' He put up his hands in mock defence. 'I know. I said no pressure.' He raised his gaze to the ceiling. 'Okay, Bessy, I'm coming. We'll leave Shanni here to make up her mind.'

'I… I'll think about it.'

'Please.'

CHAPTER FOUR

SHE cleared the dishes. She finished wiping out the fridge and replacing the few things that were actually edible. Then she made her way through the darkened house to her bedroom.

She could hear footsteps upstairs, pacing back and forth. There was a soft male rumble. Pierce was comforting Bessy.

He was a bachelor. He'd taken on five children he didn't know. The enormity of what he'd done left her gasping.

'He's a very nice boy,' she told the dark, and she giggled.

But then her giggle faded. This was deadly serious. Pierce was fighting to keep these kids together. The least she could do was help.

But she didn't do kids. And she had a career to resurrect.

'You've stuffed up big time,' she told the dark. She walked over to the bed and gave a tentative bounce.

This must be the master bedroom. Pierce had let Maureen have the master bedroom?

Why had he bought a house with so many bedrooms? Had he thought of having a big family himself?

He really was…

A hunk. The thought of him pacing back and forth above her head with a baby cradled against his shoulder…

It was a very, very sexy image.

Whoa. 'That's exactly the attitude that gets you into trouble over and over again,' she scolded herself. 'And that's the scary thing about staying. He's extraordinarily attractive and he's up to his eyeballs in domesticity, and you feel sorry for him, and if you're not careful you'll be installed as chief cook and bottle washer with your only payment a bit of snogging on the side.

'He hasn't got time for snogging.

'Just as well.' She said it out loud.

His footsteps paused right above her head. 'I know it itches,' she heard him say. 'But we all need to sleep.'

A whimper.

'In with me again? Bess, we need to cut this out.'

He was more than a hunk, she decided. He was gorgeous.

And up to his neck in kids.

'So go to bed and stop thinking about him,' she told herself, and crossed to the window to pull the blind.

There was a cow six inches from her nose.

She managed to stay silent. The cow gazed in, and she felt extraordinarily pleased with herself that she hadn't yelped. The last thing she needed was for Pierce to come racing downstairs because she was scared of a cow. The cow was outside and she was inside.

Fine.

It was a very large cow.

Its face was enormous. And its eyes looked sort of wild. It wasn't placidly gazing. Its head was moving back and forth, as if it was terrified.

Did cows get scared?

Upstairs Bessy started howling again. Obviously not even the enticement of sleeping with Pierce could placate her.

There was a moment's silence as Bessy paused for breath to start the next yowl.

'Git out.'

For a moment she thought she was imagining things. Who…?

'Git out of our garden.' It was a child's voice, yelling. It sounded like an attempt to be commanding, but there was an edge of fear showing through.

She pulled up the window—just a little—not so much that the cow could put its head in. The cow had shifted aside, turning to face whoever was shouting.

The moon was almost full. She could see clearly into the garden.

It was seven-year-old Donald. The skinny one with the scared eyes and the look that said he distrusted the world. The rest of the kids had enjoyed painting this afternoon, but Donald had painted like he was performing a duty. He looked like a kid who was waiting for the axe to fall.

'What are you doing out there?' she called, and the cow turned to look at her. Still with the wild eyes.

It was a really big cow.

Huge.

'It shouldn't be in the garden,' Donald said, struggling to sound brave. 'Someone's left the gate open. I saw it out the window. It'll eat the rose Pierce planted when our mum died.' He hiccupped on a sob, bravery disappearing. 'I'm shooing it out the gate, but it won't go.'

'Donald, you're too little be shooing cows. I'll get Pierce.'

'He's busy with Bessy.' She saw his small shoulders stiffen in resolution. 'And I'm not too little. I can do it.'

'But—'

'Git on out,' Donald said, but he'd moved backwards behind a camellia bush and she could no longer see him.

Despite his defiance, he sounded terrified.

Cows are harmless, she told herself, recalling the words of her farming-type friend.

Right.

She'd go upstairs and offer to take Bessy while Pierce sorted this, she thought, but Bessy's howls were becoming frantic.

Two perils. Crying baby. Or cow.

Each equally daunting.

'Shoo,' Donald yelled but the cow didn't move.

She could do this. Shanni Jefferson, cowgirl.

Right.

'Donald, hop up on the veranda,' she yelled out the window. 'I'll cope with the cow.'

She sounded decisive, she thought, pleased with the way her words had come out. In charge. A new life skill coming up. It was lucky she was still dressed in jeans and windcheater. Cowgirl gear.

She headed through the darkened house, towards the back door. She wouldn't mind a torch—but Donald was on his own. Finding a torch would take time. Torches were for wusses!

Outside the garden was rambling and overgrown, but the moon was almost full. Rounding the house, she could see the vague shape of the cow framed against the light from her bedroom window. It still looked seriously big.

Gigantic.

How big did cows get?

She couldn't see Donald.

The veranda at the front of the house started just past her bedroom window. Donald wasn't on the veranda.

She could see where the cow had come from. There was a gate leading to the paddocks. It was wide open.

Where there was one cow, there were likely to be more cows. She looked round nervously, expecting more shadows.

Nothing. So… One cow. And Donald?

'Shoo.' Donald's voice came from the camellias.

The cow was looking away from her. It was moving towards the sound of Donald's voice. Pacing. Shaking its head.

It was so big… So big…

Something winged past her ear and stung. Whatever it was must have struck the cow, as the creature jolted, rearing back as if terrified.

'Donald,' she yelled, finally admitting to herself that she was really, really scared. Whatever Jules had told her about cows being harmless, suddenly she didn't believe a word of it. And what had hit her ear? 'Donald!'

The creature was lowering its massive head. It was concentrating every inch of its enormous being on something behind the camellias. It was pacing.

'Sh… Shanni…' It was a terrified whisper, and to the creature it seemed like a starter's gun. The creature heaved itself forward.

'Donald!' she screamed, and she launched herself blindly out of the darkness, lashing out at the shape in front of her.

Afterwards she couldn't believe she'd done it. The creature was launching itself at the sound of Donald's quavering voice. Shanni hit it side on, walloping into it with such force that it was shifted off course.

'Get inside,' she screamed. 'Run. Donald, run.'

'Pierce!' the child screamed. 'Pierce.'

Good call, she thought, but she wasn't actually thinking all that clearly.

The creature was swinging aside, snorting, rearing back...

Dear God...

What did bullfighters do?

They ran. If they had any sense, they ran.

But the creature had a one-track mind. It was swinging back to face Donald again.

Donald was trying to scramble onto the veranda, but the veranda was almost three feet above the garden and the steps were too far away. He'd never pull himself up.

It was moving again. 'No!' She launched herself forward again, screaming, smashing her fist into the side of the creature's head.

It flung round so fast she couldn't move to avoid it.

'Pierce!' Donald screamed again.

It had horns. She grabbed a horn and clung. Stupidly. Crazily.

It swung so wildly she let go, tossed aside, landing in a limp heap four feet from the creature's head.

It backed to see what was attacking it, finally deflected from Donald.

She rolled sideways, trying to find her feet.

It was moving. It was moving…

'No!' She pushed herself fiercely sideways, rolling into the undergrowth. Oh, God…

A horn hit her shoulder with a sickening thud. She felt a crash and a fierce jabbing pain but she kept rolling. 'No!'

But suddenly there was another player.

'Get. Get, get, get.' It was a man's fierce shout. Pierce. He was launching himself down from the veranda, yelling at the top of his lungs. His yells were filling the night.

She was flinching for the next impact, but it didn't come.

'Get, get, get!'

She rolled again, deeper into shadow, and dared to look out. The creature was staring in at her, hitting the ground with its hoof, gathering momentum for another rush. But Pierce was beside it, silhouetted against the moon, swinging something that looked like a rifle.

Shoot it, she thought, but she was too dazed to think more.

'Move, move, move!' Pierce's yells could have woken the dead. He was powering into the creature's path, putting himself between Shanni and everything else, lashing out like his rifle was a scythe.

The creature swung to face him.

'Get, get, get!' Pierce was giving it no time to think. He was right in its face, swinging his weapon, smashing forward. He was yelling, hitting, pushing...

The creature backed. Backed some more.

Pierce was following it, right on top of it, giving it no quarter.

Back. Back out of the garden. Back...

The creature turned, confused, beaten, lumbering towards the gate. And as it did Shanni saw...a dangly bit underneath.

As if she'd needed confirmation.

It was through the gate now. The great wooden gate swung closed with a crash. The rifle was tossed aside.

'Donald, are you okay? Donald...' Pierce was striding through the garden, hauling himself up on the veranda, tugging Donald into his arms. 'What the hell...?'

'Shanni,' Donald quavered.

'Are you okay?' She could see their shapes on the veranda, huddled together.

'Yes.' It was a whisper. 'It hit Shanni. She's down there.'

'Shanni?' He put Donald away at arm's length. 'Where?'

'It was trying to hit her. I... I think it did.'

'Stay there, mate. Don't move.' He was jumping down from the veranda, crashing through the undergrowth, searching in the direction the bull had been aiming for. 'Shanni. Shanni, where are you? Shanni…' His voice cracked in desperation.

She had to speak. 'I'm here,' she managed, but she had to try again because her voice didn't quite work. 'H…here.'

Then, as he swore and swore again, as he dived beneath the undergrowth, as he knelt beside her and swore even more, as he put his hand on her shoulder and felt the warm stickiness of blood and stopped swearing—stopped even breathing—she asked the question she most wanted to know.

'Why don't you use test tubes?'

They were all in the kitchen. Everyone. Wendy was sitting in the rocker by the fire, cradling Bessy. Donald was standing about as close to Wendy as he could get. Abby was at Donald's feet, hugging his legs. Bryce had decreed everyone needed cocoa and was making it. Very slowly. His hands were shaking.

Shanni was doing a lot of shaking herself.

Pierce had ripped her windcheater even more than the bull had. He'd exposed a long, shallow graze that ran from her underarm almost to her throat. He had a bowl of soapy water and he was washing it and swearing under his breath.

'Not in front of the children,' she whispered.

'I locked that gate,' he muttered, towelling her

shoulder with care. 'It was padlocked. I'm not a fool. The chain's been cut.'

'Clever bull.'

'The bull's sausages,' he told her. Then he shook his head. 'No. I don't know what's going on, but Clyde's normally even sookier than the cows he services. There's things going on I don't understand.' He was inspecting her wound, his face grim. 'I don't think this needs stitching, but maybe we need to get you checked out.'

'You're thinking of leaving the kids while we go to the nearest hospital?'

'If we need to…'

'We don't need.'

'But—'

'Just put a bandage on it,' she said. 'Bandages will make me better.' She looked down into Abby's huge eyes. 'Don't bandages make things better?'

'And jelly beans,' Abby said. 'There's bandages in the bathroom.' She hugged Donald's legs a bit more and then rose stoutly to her feet, almost offering herself as personal sacrifice. 'I'll get them. But I don't know about jelly beans.'

It was a big deal for Abby, going through the house by herself, Shanni thought. These kids…

They were the bravest kids. She could see exactly why Pierce didn't want them separated.

'Do we have jelly beans?' she demanded.

'No,' Pierce said ruefully. 'Omission on my part.'

'No jelly beans?' She was watching Donald. 'What sort of a dad is this who doesn't supply jelly beans?'

'He's okay,' Donald said diffidently.

'Yes, but he needs help.' She swallowed. Her shoulder was, in truth, really painful, but this was no time for whinging. Donald looked so white he appeared to be about to pass out. He needed a mum, she thought. He needed someone to cuddle him until the terror passed. But there was something about the set of his small shoulders that said he wouldn't be accepting cuddles. Not from her. Not from Pierce. He was holding himself aloof.

'Pen and paper,' she said. 'Donald, fast.'

'What... Why?'

Abby reappeared with Elastoplast. Pierce started cutting and sticking. Ouch, ouch and ouch, thought Shanni.

'A list,' she said stoutly. 'Top of the list—jelly beans.'

'Next on the list—broom,' Pierce said and she blinked.

'We need a broom?'

'I broke the top off slamming the gate home.'

'You had a broom? I thought you had a rifle.'

'A broom.'

'My hero,' she muttered. 'Hero with broomstick. What a man.'

'Sorry.' But he was smiling. She'd made him smile, she thought, and it felt okay.

'So, broom,' she told Donald. 'And the makings of hot dogs.'

'Why hot dogs?' Pierce asked.

'Because I feel like a hot dog and I'm wounded. Wounded people can ask for whatever they want.'

'I like hot dogs,' Donald said cautiously.

'I think they're made from bulls,' she told him, and she grinned. 'Double rations of hot dogs just as soon as we can get to the store.'

'That might be next week,' Pierce warned her. 'I get groceries delivered on Monday.'

'Monday's too far. If the stores were open now I'd want my hot dog now.' She sighed. 'But I'm willing—at great personal sacrifice—to wait till tomorrow. Wendy and I can take care of the house. You can take Donald and do a shopping expedition. A hot dog hunt.'

'Does that mean you're staying for a bit?' Wendy asked, and it seemed like the whole room held its breath.

Was she? She gazed round the room and saw five needful faces. Six if she counted Pierce, who was looking like he was trying to look uninterested.

Needful, too, she thought, but then that was suddenly a dangerous thought.

Ware sympathy, she told herself sternly, but she

was still staying. 'If it's okay with you,' she said diffidently, and not looking at Pierce. 'I've come here nursing shattered pride, and now I have a broken shoulder to recover from as well. Recovering might take some time.'

It took time to settle everyone. Shanni sat in the big rocker by the fire while Pierce put his brood to bed. The children's bedrooms were upstairs as well. She could hear them talking in muted tones. Kids' questions. Pierce's rumbling answers. Bessy's plaintive whinging. More rumbles. A child's voice—Wendy's—sounding bossy.

She should go to bed, Shanni thought, but she was still feeling shaky. The gentle rocking of the old chair and the crackling of the flames inside the stove were infinitely comforting.

Silence fell upstairs. She might go to sleep where she was, and that didn't seem a bad option. Preferable to going to a strange bed.

But some plans were doomed to failure.

'Why aren't you in bed?' It was Pierce, standing in the doorway, staring across at her in concern.

'I'm going,' she said without much conviction. 'As soon as I'm warm.'

'It's a warm night.'

'I guess it is. I just got cold.'

He looked worried. But he was standing in the

doorway, not coming further. 'You want more of that whisky?'

'No. I...I shouldn't.'

'Me neither. But it's scary how much I want some.' He shook his head. 'Hell, Shanni, I'm sorry.'

'You said the gate was locked.'

'That's what I can't understand.' He hesitated, but he still wasn't coming further into the room. 'I've just double checked. The chain's been cut with bolt cutters. And someone's stirred Clyde up. I'm not threatening to turn him into sausages any more. He's standing against the fence, trembling almost as much as you are. There's a series of tiny puncture wounds along his flank. I'd suspect something like a peashooter's been used to hurt him. Normally if you opened Clyde's gate he wouldn't even notice it was open. But, if you opened it and started shooting pellets at him, he'd get terrified. He'd lumber into the garden, and if he kept hurting and he didn't understand why then he'd be likely to attack anything that moved.'

She was staring at him, horrified. 'But that's... that's criminal. That's awful.'

'They'll be aiming at me,' he said grimly. 'They'll assume it'd be me who'd go out and check on cattle loose in the garden. They'd never assume it'd be a seven-year-old.'

'Do they hate you that much?'

'It's not hate,' he said grimly. 'It's just they don't know me. I'm a weekend millionaire who stopped a factory going ahead that the community needed. The fact that no one warned me is irrelevant. And now, as well as being rich and stupid and forcing the community to lose its factory, I'm a single dad who Social Welfare has in its sights for child neglect. Yeah, they'd like me to pack up and leave.'

'So why don't you?' she asked cautiously.

'I...'

'You could go back to your architecture in the city. The kids could go to school and to day care. You could hire a housekeeper easier in the city.'

'It won't work.' He shook his head. 'Or I'm not sure it'd work. Maybe it'll come to that, but Maureen badly wanted these kids to have space.'

She hesitated. And then she said, wise for now, 'Well, at least you have me for a bit.'

There was a baffled pause. At least, it was baffled on Shanni's part. Why the silence?

'I think I just offered to be housekeeper,' she said at last, cautiously. 'If you want me.'

'I do want you.'

It was said with such force that she blinked—and then managed a smile. 'Well, thank you.'

'I can see Ruby in you.'

That made her blink again. 'Little and dumpy and wide astern?'

He smiled at that, grimness easing. 'I'd never have said wide astern.'

'But I'm little and dumpy.'

'What you did tonight was the bravest…'

'You're saying that makes up for little and dumpy?'

He grinned. 'If I was in the market for a woman, little and dumpy would be the last way I'd describe you.'

'You're not in the market for a woman?'

'What do you think?'

'I guess you've got five kids. So you're not in the market for any more family.'

'I never wanted this much. I sure as hell don't need a wife as well.'

How had this conversation happened?

'Just lucky you told me,' she managed. 'I was already planning the bridal.'

It brought him up short. 'Hell. Shanni, I didn't mean…'

'It's okay,' she told him, relenting 'I've done enough bridal planning for a lifetime.'

'With ice-water Mike.'

'That's the one. I thought I was in love. How stupid can you be? No more relationships for me.'

'But you've told the kids.'

'That I'll stay for a bit. Yes, I have.' She took a deep breath, trying to sort things out in her head. 'I really am in trouble,' she confessed, deciding to lay it all out. 'I used every cent I had getting back to Australia, to find my parents had sublet their house. My best friend has a bedsitter smaller than your broom closet. I've been out of the country for eight years and there's no one else I can crash on. Except Ruby and her macramé ladies.'

'It's some penthouse she's in,' Pierce said. 'Forty squares of luxury overlooking Sydney Harbour.'

Shanni frowned, suddenly thinking sideways. Ruby… Ruby of the gorgeous sons. Ruby who didn't have a cent to her name, suddenly swanning in a penthouse in Sydney's most exclusive harbour-front suburb?

'You gave her the penthouse?'

'We all did. Hasn't Ruby told you about the rest of her boys?'

'Of course she has.' She remembered the photograph Ruby carried with her everywhere. Ruby, dotty old Ruby, who'd never had a penny to bless herself with, who'd spent every minute of her life devoted to her boys. 'Blake, Connor, Sam, Darcy, Dominic, Nikolai. And Pierce,' she whispered. 'Do I have them right?'

'That's us. Ruby's boys. She took us in, and she hauled every one of us up by the bootstraps. She was left with nothing. For her seventieth birthday we gave her the apartment, The stipulation is that she doesn't sell it or give it away to freeloaders, and she's no longer permitted to take in strays.'

'Not permitted?'

'It's time we started protecting her from herself. If we hadn't stipulated it, would you be in her guest room?'

'No.' She sighed. 'Well, if it wasn't for the macramé, maybe. She does have the reputation of not turning anyone out.'

'You really are desperate?'

'I can get a job. I guess. The art world's so small, though. People know my gallery failed.'

'So you'll accept this job?'

'I guess. For a bit.'

Why didn't he come into the room? she wondered. He was standing at the doorway as if afraid to come further.

'I won't bite,' she said, but he didn't smile.

'No.'

'What are you afraid of?'

'You're Ruby's niece?'

'By marriage, yes.

'Then we're practically related.'

'Family,' she agreed and waited.

'Maybe I should say right now… I don't want any sort of relationship.'

Her shoulder was hurting. It had been hurting all this while, but she'd forgotten about it for a little. Now it slammed back and it was like he'd slapped her.

'What are you saying?'

'I didn't mean…'

'You *did* mean. That's the second weird comment. Are you expecting me to jump you?'

'No, I—'

'That's good, because I'm not,' she snapped. 'I'm nuts to be here. Seriously, totally barmy. I'd be best throwing myself on the mercy of the parish or whatever indigent people do these days.'

'It's not really as bad as that.'

She glared. 'No,' she conceded. 'All I have to do is contact my parents and I'll be fine. But I'm offering to stay here.'

'Why?'

'Because Donald was going to tackle that bull all by himself rather than haul you away from his baby sister. Because Wendy's looking older than her years. Because this house is a mess—this family is a mess—and I need a job, so I might as well do one that's worth doing. You say you're wealthy?'

It was such a change of tack that he blinked. 'I... Yes.'

'Could you afford to take us all to the beach?'

'The beach?'

'You see, these kids look like they're expecting the weight of the world to descend on their heads any minute. Or maybe it's already descended. Have they been away from this place since their mother died?'

'No, but...'

'They've been sick?'

'Yes, but...'

'And it's school holidays?'

'Yes.'

'There you go, then,' she said. 'Take us away. To the beach.'

'How the hell am I going to take five kids—including one chicken-poxed baby—to the beach?'

'I'll come, too,' she said patiently. 'I like the beach. The kids are recuperating from pox, I'm recuperating from mortification and, you need to work.'

He blinked. Work. He'd practically forgotten about work.

'I can't.'

'Of course you can't work here,' she agreed. 'And the kids are so spooked that I can't see things changing. So what I suggest is that we hire two apartments for a couple of weeks.'

'Two.'

'One for you and one for me,' she said. 'Right on the beach. Somewhere luxurious. See how good I am at spending other people's money?'

'How would that work?'

'At night I'll share with the girls and you share with the boys,' she said. 'During the day the kids can stay with me, and we'll play at the beach. If we stay at a decent resort there'll be babysitters as well, and if we find one who's had the pox then we can leave Bessy a little. I could really use a week or two at the beach.'

Whoops.

Until now it hadn't been about her. She'd tried really hard to couch this in terms that said she was doing this out of the goodness of her heart.

But she'd let it out. She heard it the moment her words left her mouth, and she saw Pierce's face change.

'*You* want to go to the beach?'

'I had the flu,' she said ruefully. 'The morning I found Mike… Well, it was the start of three weeks of being sick. And every single day since then I've thought of the beach. Mum and Dad's house is on the beach north of Sydney. That's where I was headed. Then tonight I was under that blasted camellia waiting for Clyde to turn me into sausages, and all I could think of was that I hadn't made it to the beach.'

His face softened. For a moment—for just a moment—his face changed. He smiled, a lovely gentle smile that made something inside her twist.

'I could lend you money to go the beach by yourself.' Then he shook his head. 'No. After all you've done for my family today, it's not a loan. You deserve to have a holiday without us.'

'I may be dumb,' she said with dignity, shaking her head. 'But I'm hooked now. All or nothing.'

'You don't want a long-term commitment to these kids?'

'Are you kidding? Of course I don't. But a week or two at the beach while we recover…'

'It does sound…' He dug his hands deep in his

pockets and considered. What must he be seeing, she thought. A waif. A dumb, failed art curator with skin that was too pale after too long in England and three weeks of the flu. A woman who'd been rolling round in the garden fighting with a bull. Blood- and dust-spattered. Tear streaked—okay, there might just have been a few tears when no one had been looking…

'I really do need to work,' he said at last. 'I mean, yeah, I'm wealthy, but it's not bottomless. There's a project I was going to have to renege on. If I could get time on that…'

'We could stay here,' she admitted. 'But we all need to bounce a bit.'

'You mean you do.'

She tilted her chin. 'Yes,' she said. 'It's pure selfishness on my part.' But then she shook her head. 'No. I'm looking at Wendy, too. She needs—she needs to be a kid.'

'You think I don't know that?'

'So can we go to the beach?'

'How the hell can I organize…?'

'See, here's the thing,' she said, apologetically. 'I might be a failed art curator but I have a splinter skill. It's called web junkie. You put me in front of an internet connection, and I'll have us at the beach this time tomorrow. Promise.'

He stared at her. She stared back. Her shoulder hurt, she thought. And Pierce could see it. He was watching her, but there was something behind his eyes that said he was seeing further than skin deep.

The beach. Focus on the beach.

'You're on,' he said at last, so softly she hardly heard him. 'So, when the kids wake up in the morning…'

'We'll be packing for the beach. You'd better get that tyre fixed. Though I've got my dad's car. I'll follow behind. I'm not relinquishing my independence that much.'

'We'll talk about it in the morning.' At last he left the door, crossing to where she sat huddled before the fire. 'Let me help you to bed.'

'I'm fine.'

'You're still shaking.'

'I'm just not used to bulls,' she said with as much dignity as she could muster.

'No one's used to a bull like that. He could have killed you. If you hadn't gone out he may well have killed Donald.'

'Gee, that's the sort of thing to say to stop me shaking,' she muttered.

'Shanni, you're beat.' He hesitated for a moment and then shrugged, seeming to shake off whatever scruples he might be feeling. Before she knew what he intended, he bent and scooped her up into his arms, holding her close.

'What the—?'

'I'm taking you to bed,' he told her. 'But not downstairs. Yeah, that's Maureen's room. No one's been in it since she died. There's a spare bed in Wendy's room. I think you'd be better off sleeping with the kids.'

'I'm a grown woman,' she protested. 'Hey, Pierce, I'm an independent career woman. Are you putting me to bed with the children?'

'Too right I am,' he told her. 'You need company to get you to sleep.' He gave a rueful grin. 'I'd like to offer my services, but my bed's already occupied. Me and Bessy—the woman of my dreams.'

She didn't protest. He carried her into the spare bed in the girls' room. He helped her off with what remained of her windcheater. He would have helped her more, but she suddenly woke enough to be independent.

'I'm fine,' she said and suddenly the atmosphere changed. She'd let him cradle her against him as he climbed the stairs. She'd seemed to need his warmth—his strength—but suddenly there was tension.

He retreated, leaving her to it. She was confused. He could see she was confused—and so was he.

Back in his bedroom, Bessy slept, which was a mixed blessing. 'When I'm awake you might as well be awake, too,' he told her. 'When I go to sleep that's when you'll wail.' But Bessy wasn't listening. She had her chubby fist pressed into her mouth and she was seriously sucking her tiny knuckles as she seriously slept.

He should sleep himself. But too much had happened too fast. His heart rate was still up there, and it wasn't going to slow down soon.

When he'd put his hands under the camellia, searching, he'd felt the blood and for a couple of awful moments, until he'd carried her to the veranda and been able to see the extent of the damage, he'd thought the worst.

Well, his heart rate hadn't yet settled.

'I do not need someone else to worry about,' he told the sleeping Bessy. 'A waif whose boyfriend's duped her out of her livelihood, whose parents have left her stranded.'

'Are you kidding? She's a mature woman. Pushing thirty? She has to be. Did you see the way she organized the cleaning? She's not a kid.'

'It's the way she looks at me.'

Bessy stirred and grunted and waved her small fist in the air. He took it, and she wrapped her fingers around his middle finger and clung.

Domesticity closed in from all sides.

'I should never have bought this house.'

'So sell it.'

'No.'

'Well, get out of here at least. Take Miss Bossy Boots to the sea. Give us all a break.'

He sighed. Sleep was nowhere.

Miss Bossy Boots was right before him. That awful

moment when he'd dragged her out from under the bush, before he'd seen…

'That's what this is,' he told himself. 'It's horror. And gratitude. She saved Donald.'

'She's some woman.'

See, that was just the route his thoughts didn't want to take. He'd made one mistake in the past. Or two, he admitted, being ruthlessly honest.

One was buying this place. It had been a dumb-ass romantic gesture. His brothers had made him see how stupid it was.

The second was his response to Maureen. *Maureen, if you're dying… Hell of course you can bring the kids here. I'll take care of you.*

And now his life was down the toilet. His work was a disaster. If he didn't get this project in…

Miss Bossy Boots had a point. Two apartments.

But the kids would want to be with him. Or he'd worry if they weren't. There had to be a solution.

Beach.

Kids.

Castle.

He sat up so fast that Bessy woke and glared, then grinned in the moonlight and held up her arms for a cuddle.

'Right,' he said, hugging Bessy obligingly and throwing back the covers. 'Let's go look on the internet. Only I'm looking for a very specific place. A place I already know about. A place where I can back off and leave the emotion to trained professionalism.'

Including how he felt towards Shanni? How he might be feeling, but he was admitting nothing...

'It's a package deal,' he told Bessy. 'Ruby says it's a place of miracles. Let's hope she's right.'

CHAPTER FIVE

SHANNI went to sleep in a skinny kid's bed, with Wendy and Abby sleeping almost within touching distance.

She woke and the kids' beds were empty. She could hear voices from downstairs.

The room was empty.

She lay and stared at the ceiling, watching early morning sunbeams flicker on the wooden beams of the ceiling. This was the loveliest old farmhouse. She could see why Pierce had wanted it. It was a home.

The home he'd never had.

But he didn't want attachment. He didn't want marriage. It was like he'd bought the place just so he could bring up stray kids.

Maureen must have been so relieved to find him.

Pierce.

A nice boy...

He was nice, she thought, still half asleep, drifting in the warmth and comfort of her tiny bed. He was really nice.

Yeah, and she'd thought Mike was nice, she told herself harshly as she realized where her thoughts were taking her. She needed to haul them right back under control. Her judgement in men was seriously flawed. She needed time out—at least a year or so before she'd even think about dipping a toe in the water again.

And there'd be no dipping of toes with someone like Pierce. He had five kids. It'd be like jumping over Niagara Falls.

Right. So stay sensible. She gave herself a mental shake and rolled onto her side, preliminary to getting out of bed.

Mistake.

Last night she'd had what she thought was a grazed shoulder. Now… Maybe it was a compound fracture. Plus gangrene. Or something worse.

She whimpered and rolled onto her back.

'Ouch!' said a voice from the door. She looked over, and there was Pierce. He had a couple of kids behind him. He was smiling.

He'd shaved, she thought inconsequentially. He was wearing linen pants and a green polo shirt with a little alligator icon on the chest. He looked like he'd stepped straight off the cover of *Vogue*.

He made her feel…

'It's nine o'clock,' Wendy said from behind him. 'Pierce said it's time to wake you.'

'I've made a doctor's appointment for you in half an hour,' Pierce said apologetically. 'Or we would have let you sleep longer.'

'A doctor's appointment?'

'The man from the garage brought a new tyre for Mum's wagon,' Bryce said. 'So we can come with you.'

'There's a little seat in the back,' Wendy added. 'So it's a seven-seater. Isn't that lucky?'

'Cos there's seven of us,' Abby added importantly. 'You want to hear me count?'

'How's the arm?' Pierce asked.

That was the only thing that she could make sense of. She lay back and looked at him, solidly looked at him, at his anxious face, at the amazing good looks of the man, at his worried frown and the way his brow just puckered at the edges.

'I feel like I need painkillers,' she confessed. 'But then I already feel like I've taken them. Giddy.'

'You do need to see a doctor.'

'Maybe,' she said cautiously.

'Right, then. Will you stay in bed? I can carry you to the car.'

'I'm getting up,' she said indignantly.

'You're sure?'

'Yes.'

'Do you need help to get dressed?'

'No.' In fact—and she wasn't admitting this for

quids—she'd gone to sleep in her bra and knickers. It had hurt too much to take her bra off.

'Wendy, stay and help her,' Pierce ordered. 'The rest of you, breakfast. Bryce is on toast duty. There'll be half a ton toasted by the time you get down.' He smiled at her, that heart-stopping smile that made her heart, well, not stop, but it was a near-run thing. 'Take care of her, Wendy.'

'I…'

'Oh, and we've organized the beach,' he added as if it was an afterthought. 'Your offer of internet hunting was noted with gratitude, but we've found our own place.'

'We're going to a castle,' Bryce said, sounding awed. 'A castle at the beach. The castle at Dolphin Bay. So we're having hot dogs today and beach tomorrow as soon as Pierce has found someone to take care of the farm.'

She felt like she was caught in a tidal wave, washing her along with a momentum that didn't allow her time for breath. Not that she wanted to breathe. Her shoulder hurt. Boy, did it hurt. It hurt all the time she dressed and all the time she had breakfast, and it hurt as she walked out to the car.

She was aware of Pierce's eyes on her every step of the way, so she fought it. She grinned at the antics of the kids—she tried to keep up with the backchat—

but in the car she subsided into blessed silence. She didn't speak again until they pulled up outside the doctor's surgery.

Pierce was out of the car almost as soon as they stopped, hauling open the passenger door, helping her out, his expression grave.

'Well done you,' he said softly, and he put his finger under her chin in a gesture of reassurance. 'We should have called the ambulance last night. What a hero.'

'I'm not a hero,' she managed, but she whished he wouldn't do this. Look at her like this. Touch her...

She'd thought he was fabulous when he was fifteen. He'd grown...*fabulouser*?

'Did you get any sleep at all?'

'I was jet lagged,' she managed. 'I would have slept if I'd been on the rack.'

'And that's how you feel this morning? Like you spent the night on the rack?'

'A bit.' He was helping the kids out of the car now. 'Um, where are you guys going?'

'We're coming to the doctor's with you,' Bryce explained.

'You have to be kidding.' She stared at them like they were out of their collective minds.

'If you get an injection you need someone to hold your hand,' Abby said, and put out her hand in offering.

'I'll be fine,' Shanni said, backing away. What was she getting into?

'Okay. We'll fetch our mended tyre and do the supermarket shopping while we wait,' Pierce told her, grinning. 'But I want the truth about what the doctor says.'

There was no way Shanni was giving him the truth about what the doctor said. Because after a cursory glance at her arm— 'Badly bruised, lacerations, you'd expect it to be painful for a few days, I'll prescribe painkillers.'—the doctor started in on a subject he cared about more than Shanni.

'What the hell is that idiot about, letting cattle wander? The man's a lunatic.'

There was such dislike in the doctor's voice that she flinched. 'The bolt to the paddock was cut,' she said, confused. 'It's criminal negligence, or worse, but it's not Pierce's fault. Pierce should be calling in the police.'

'It's criminal negligence,' he agreed. 'But it's not Mr MacLachlan who should be calling the police. It's you. If he let bulls graze without protective barriers…' He grimaced. 'It's the last straw. There's no way I'm letting those children stay at risk.' He reached for the phone.

Something was seriously screwy.

She put her hand firmly on the telephone, forcing him to replace it.

'Indulge me,' she said slowly. 'Charge me for a

long consultation if you must. But I've been employed as a nanny for Pierce's children. I need you to be honest. As one professional to another, tell me why you think Pierce MacLachlan is a bad parent.'

Supermarket shopping was Pierce's least favourite pastime. Not that these kids were ill behaved—on the contrary, they'd had such a hard time while their mother had been ill that every time he put anything but bread and pasta in the trolley it seemed an occasion for general rejoicing. But supermarkets in small country towns were full of small country people. That's what they were, he thought, as he passed one matron after another with her nose raised in sniffy disapproval. Small minded and mean.

Where was the legendary country hospitality? Nowhere. It was a great idea of Shanni's to go to the beach. Maybe he should move the whole lot of them there permanently.

Though wherever he went he'd probably get this level of disapproval, he thought. Single dad with a gaggle of disparate kids.

'Can you tell me where the hot-dog rolls are?' he asked a middle-aged woman stacking shelves, and she practically bristled.

'Aisle ten,' she snapped.

'It's aisle three.' Shanni's voice shocked them all. It was so loud it stopped everyone in their tracks.

He swivelled to see where the voice was coming from.

Shanni was at the end of their aisle, and she was holding a microphone. The mike was obviously the one used for messages such as, 'Gimme a price on the broccoli.'

Shanni seemed to have purloined it for her personal use.

'I can see bread from here,' she boomed. 'Hot-dog rolls in aisle three. The lady's telling lies.'

'I never—' The shelf-stacking lady's jaw dropped almost to her ankles.

'There's a lot of that happening,' Shanni said conversationally, and then, as the girl at the checkout counter made a grab for her microphone, Shanni shook her head, smiled sweetly and stepped sideways.

'I need it, there's a pet,' she said. 'I have a very important announcement.'

'What…?' the girl demanded but she was too late. Shanni was in full flow. She was standing in front of the middle register, giving her a clear view of almost everyone in their various aisles. Which was a lot of people. This must be pay day or something, Pierce thought, bewildered. The supermarket was packed.

'Many of you know Pierce MacLachlan,' she said conversationally, and he had a frantic urge to surge forward and grab the microphone. But he couldn't quite get his legs to work.

'He bought a local farm,' Shanni went on. 'For those who don't know, it's a neat little farm with a fabulous farmhouse. Pierce is a city architect. I'm assuming he saw the farm advertised in a city paper. He made an appointment with the agent. He liked what he saw and he bought it. No problem. Except there was a corporation negotiating to buy it so they could set up a factory here. The factory then had to be built on a site near the next town, which means many of you now have to pay an additional cartage to get your milk there. Pierce is sorry about that, but it's not his fault. He didn't know. If you're blaming him, then it's totally unfair. Unchristian, really.'

There was absolute silence. Customers in Pierce's aisle turned and stared at Pierce and his brood of kids. Everyone else stared at Shanni.

'So Pierce moved in,' she said. 'And, while everyone was tut-tutting in disapproval, he invited Maureen to stay. Maureen was Pierce's foster sister. She had four kids and was pregnant with the fifth. She was also dying.'

There was a general intake of breath. An assistant manager—a guy of about nineteen wearing more grease than a fish shop—was striding towards Shanni looking as if he knew what to do with anyone who was interfering with *his* microphone. But an older woman grabbed him by the arm and held him back.

'Leave her be, Dwayne.'

'Mum, she can't—'

'Shush. I want to hear.'

'Anyway,' Shanni said, ignoring Dwayne as insignificant to her story, 'Here was Maureen with her kids. In desperate trouble. Her background is irrelevant. I'm not asking you to judge Maureen. We can't. For Maureen died eight months ago.'

'We know this,' someone called out.

'Then if you do you should be ashamed of yourselves,' Shanni snapped. 'I gave you the benefit of the doubt, that you didn't know the facts. So I'm repeating them. These kids… They're fantastic kids. You can't imagine. Wendy's eleven. She's held her brothers and sisters together like the little mother hen she is. All the kids—Wendy and Bryce and Donald and Abby and Bessy—every single one of them deserves a medal for the care they took of their mother and the care they've taken of each other. But of course, there are five of them. When Maureen was ill there was no one to look after them. Social Welfare knew Maureen was dying. They were rightly concerned. Maureen was terrified they'd be separated. She begged Pierce to help. Not being the children's father, Pierce could do little. But Pierce has a big farm and a bigger heart. He thought if he was the kids' stepdad then he might just be able to keep them together. So he and Maureen married.'

There was silence. The locals hadn't figured this

part of the story. They'd preferred juicier versions, Pierce thought. Various kids with various parents, kept for whatever nefarious purpose they might like to imagine.

'Do you really think Social Welfare would let Pierce keep the children if they don't think he has the best interests of the kids at heart?' Shanni demanded, and there was even more silence.

'You know, I was brought up in the city,' Shanni said. 'My mum got glandular fever when I was seven, and she was ill for months. I remember that time as scary, but you know what? My dad and I never had to cook. Our local community—city folk—used to turn up at our place with food. My school organized a roster. It makes me cry now, more than twenty years on, to think of all those big-hearted people.

'But you,' she said, lowering her voice. She didn't have to worry about it so much now. She had the absolute attention of every single person in the supermarket. 'These kids go to your kids' school. You've known Pierce was in trouble. But all he gets from you, his community, is more and more reports forcing Social Welfare to keep on checking.'

She took a deep breath. 'All these kids have had chicken pox. Now Bessy has it. I know, she's in the supermarket when she shouldn't be, but there's no choice. Even with me helping. Yesterday Pierce stayed up all night with an ill child, but he had to take

Bessy to the doctor. He was so tired, he went to sleep in his car while waiting for a prescription. The kids were safe at home with me, but he got reported. He got home to face yet another check. Then last night someone decided Welfare weren't doing their job, the job someone here seems to want, which is running Pierce and the kids out of town. So they decided to help things along.'

'Shanni,' Pierce said and started forward, but Wendy grabbed his shirt and clung.

'Let her say it, Dad,' she said. 'These people don't like it.'

'So someone let our bull into the garden,' Shanni said. Her voice was strained now, like she was having trouble going on. 'Not only that, but whoever it was stirred Clyde up, wounding him with a peashooter over and over again until he was vicious and uncontrolled. I guess whoever it was imagined that it'd be Pierce who went outside when he heard a bull in the garden, but we still have a sick baby. Pierce was upstairs with a howling Bessy. So Donald...' she motioned to Donald '...our seven-year-old, who like every one of his siblings is brave and resolute and desperate to do the right thing, went out to tackle the bull on his own.'

There was a general gasp. Horror. But the lady who'd been stocking the shelves was looking at them differently. Appalled.

'I'm an old friend of Pierce, and I've come to help. I heard Donald in the garden,' Shanni said into the silence. 'I got there just before the bull charged him.' She motioned to the sling the doctor had put her arm in. 'I ended up with a wounded shoulder. But if I hadn't been there…' She broke off.

'But I was,' she said softly.

'Shanni, leave this,' Pierce said. He put Wendy aside and started walking up the aisle towards her.

'Oh, I'm leaving it,' she said, and she managed to smile at him. 'We're all leaving. We're going to the beach for a holiday. Pierce has had this place up to his ears, and I don't blame him. But in a couple of weeks we'll be back. To put the place on the market…'

'Shanni?'

'You can't keep the farm if these people keep de-monizing you,' she said softly. 'So all I'm doing is laying the facts before everyone.' She took a deep breath and then beamed, switching channels. 'Okay, everyone. Enough from me. You were in the middle of a riveting announcement of a red-hot special in laundry detergents. Dwayne, over to you.' And she handed over the mike, just as Pierce reached her.

He stopped just before her. She was smiling, but her eyes were wary. Worried.

'I had to do it, Pierce,' she whispered. 'When the doctor told me what scum you were, what everyone here thought, I damn near slapped him.' Her smile firmed a little. 'But then I would have had to slap everyone here, too, and I'd probably end up in jail, and I want to go to the beach. Can we still go to the beach, Pierce, or are you mad at me?'

'I'm mad at you.'

'How badly is your shoulder hurt, miss?' It was Dwayne's mother. She looked white-faced and frightened. There were a few white faces around, Pierce thought. How many people had been in on the Clyde plan?

'It's mostly just bruised,' Shanni assured her.

'When are you going to the beach?'

'Tomorrow.'

'Then you're not to cook tonight,' the lady said, and suddenly she'd turned and grabbed the microphone from her son. 'I'm on casserole tonight,' she boomed into the microphone. 'Dora, can you make one of your apple strudels?'

'And I'll make a hamper they can take with them,' someone called.

'We don't need—'

'I think we need,' Dwayne's mother told the supermarket grimly. 'I think a whole lot of us need a lot more than you do.'

They drove home in silence, Shanni in the front passenger seat and the kids packed into the back. For the life of him Pierce couldn't think of what to say. She'd blown him away. She'd been a virago, protecting her young with every ounce of her being.

She was a failed owner of an art gallery.

How could this woman fail at anything? For a moment he almost felt sorry for the stupid ex-boy-friend who'd betrayed her. Mike was lucky he'd only got a bucket of iced water.

He grinned.

'What's so funny?'

'I was thinking of Mike.'

'Of Mike?'

'And iced water. And microphones. I'm thinking maybe we need to get you boxing lessons. Slugging might be easier.'

'Not half as satisfying,' she said, and she smiled back.

'There is that.' He hesitated. 'Shanni, I'm really grateful.'

'I know you are,' she said smugly. 'That's why I did it.' Her smile faded. 'You know, it's occurred to me that if you're taking the kids to the beach then you don't actually need me.'

'Pardon?'

'This castle. I asked the doctor about it. After I yelled at him he started being a sweetie. We looked Dolphin Bay castle up on the internet. It's a refuge where disadvantaged kids get a holiday, and their carers do, too. There's more than enough staff to take the kids off your hands while you get your work done. I could…' She took a deep breath. 'I could go find somewhere else to stay.' But then she brightened. 'Or I could stay at the farm by myself. I could paint. Someone has to babysit Clyde.'

'But you have to come,' said Donald from the back seat.

'What if there are bulls?' Abby demanded. 'We need you to look after Donald.'

'Yes,' said Donald.

'We certainly need you, and I've found a Clyde-sitter,' Pierce said with a sidelong glance at his passenger. She was looking weary. It'd been a hell of a day yesterday. The bull's attack must have taken its toll. Yet her behaviour in the supermarket… It had been amazing.

Ruby would have fought like that, he thought, and he smiled.

'You keep having private jokes,' Shanni complained, and he tried to stop smiling. But she sounded so righteous that he wanted to smile all over again.

'You remind me of Ruby.'

'I love my Aunty Ruby,' she said warmly. But then she frowned. 'But I told you—stop saying that. She's short and dumpy.'

'And you're short and cuddly.' It was out before he realized what he'd intended to say. He hadn't intended to say it. Had he?

'I don't do cuddles,' she said.

'No?'

'Why not?' asked Wendy.

'Cos I had a boyfriend who was a rat, and I've promised I'll never cuddle anyone again.'

'Our Mum said Pierce didn't do cuddles,' Abby piped up. 'We had to teach him.'

'Kids' cuddles are different to adult cuddles.' Pierce knew he sounded desperate but that was how he was feeling.

'Why didn't you do cuddles?' Shanni asked, interested. Then she remembered something. 'Ruby says all her boys are emotionally crippled.'

'Gee, thanks.'

'There's one thing I can't understand.'

'What's that?' He sounded cautious, but who could blame him?

'Why did you buy your farm?'

The question caught him unprepared. He had no answer.

'You didn't know about Maureen and the kids before you bought it, did you?' she asked.

'Um, no.'

'You hadn't heard and decided to be super-nice?'

'I'm not super-nice.'

'No?' She screwed up her nose, deep in thought. 'You were working in Sydney on your super architect projects that earn you megabucks. You decided you wanted a weekend getaway, so you looked around here. And lo—a five-bedroom farmhouse. Two living rooms. Three bathrooms. Three dog houses. Have you ever owned a dog?'

'No.'

'There you go, then. Do you have lots of friends and relations?'

He hesitated. 'Only Ruby.'

'And the boys. Your foster brothers. Ruby's boys.' She smiled a little at that. 'Ruby thinks the world of you guys. Though you've blotted your copybook with the apartment.'

'What do you mean?'

'Buying her a fabulous apartment that she can't share. Whose cork-brained idea was that?'

'Not mine,' he admitted.

There was a lengthy silence. The kids didn't understand where the conversation was going, but they were good kids. They were content to listen.

'So,' Shanni said at last. She sank back into her seat, and he had the feeling she would have crossed her arms if she didn't have an arm in a sling. Judgement had been pronounced.

'You sound like the secrets of the universe have been revealed.'

'They have,' she said in tones of satisfaction. 'Aunty Ruby always said you were a nice boy.'

'I bet she says that about us all.'

'No. She had tags. I don't know you all, but she

has you categorized. The silent one. The dangerous one. The wild one. The deep one.'

'And I'm just nice.'

'She said it in the kindest way. She thinks the world of you.' She hesitated. 'Aunty Ruby says you see nothing of your own family.'

'No.' Short. Clipped. Brusque. Intended to give her a message which she clearly didn't receive.

'Okay.' She looked sideways at him. 'So, you bought your farm for Ruby?'

'I didn't.'

'No, not specifically, cos she'd never have taken it. But if you had a great big farmhouse that was rattlingly empty, and Ruby knew it was there and some kid or other was in trouble, she'd have filled it up. I bet that's what you were thinking. Only Maureen got in first and filled it before Ruby could.'

'It wasn't for Ruby.' But he knew he didn't sound convincing.

'Maybe it was in your subconscious, but I bet it was there. But then the rest of the boys had their great idea about giving Ruby an apartment for herself. But you knew she'd hate it.'

'I didn't know.'

'Of course you did, because you're the nice one. But you were stuck then, cos of course you couldn't be the only one who wouldn't give Ruby the apartment. And you've got five kids who you know Ruby would adore to have as pseudo-grand-kids, but of course the rest of Ruby's boys would think you were lower than the low if you foisted them on her.'

'What's "foist"?' Bryce asked.

'Let Ruby near you,' Pierce said desperately. 'I can't.'

'Which is why you told her you had one baby and only one. You knew she'd never be able to resist more.'

'She couldn't resist one. I had to practically strait-jacket her to stop her coming. I didn't want to tell her that much, but I needed my foster brother Blake to help with the legal stuff. We were staying with Ruby at the time and she overheard. She knew I was hiding something. So I told Ruby one baby.'

'And you told Ruby you didn't want her?'

'This is too damned convoluted,' he growled. 'Plus it's not your business.'

'I don't want to meet any more bulls,' she explained. 'No more unpleasant surprises. But, mean-while, you don't need me at Dolphin Bay.'

'I do,' he insisted.

'Why?'

'Because you need a damned good rest. Any fool can see that.'

'I'm your employee,' she said gently. 'Not someone you have to fuss over.'

'No, but you don't have any place else to go.'

'You could sign one of Ruby's dumb visitor

agreements and I could stay there. I could put up with the macramé.'

'You'd tell her all about me.'

'I might,' she admitted. 'Not that I'd want to, but no one can tell lies to Ruby. She sees right through you.'

'So come to the castle. Maybe you can paint.'

'Maybe I can,' she said, cheering up. 'I need to conquer cows' legs.'

'You studied art at university?'

'I did and all,' she said mournfully. 'But it hasn't fitted me very well for an alternative career. I can discuss with gravitas the powerful influences affecting post-modern gothic pastoralism on twentieth-century neoconservatist abstracts—but I can't paint a cows' leg. Wendy does a neater one. Maybe I should become the world's best housekeeper and be done with it.' She swivelled round and grinned at Wendy. 'But I'm trying painting first. So it's a contest. If I get to go to the beach, we'll see who paints legs best at the end.'

'We'll paint fish at the beach,' Abby said.

'Fish legs, then.'

'Mermaids,' Wendy said, and giggled.

Wendy giggling?

It was such an astonishing sound that it almost had Pierce driving off the road. He hadn't heard Wendy giggle since her mother had died.

This woman was…

A godsend. Nothing more, he told himself, suddenly finding he needed to give himself a stern reminder of barriers. She was great for the kids.

She was cuddly.

He didn't do cuddly. He didn't do relationships.

Except, maybe, with Ruby.

Ruby's husband had been a foster kid himself, physically scarred from years of childhood neglect. When he'd died young Ruby had declared her life mission was to rescue boys. There were too many children in the world to take them all, she declared, so she restricted herself to gawky adolescent males, and she loved them to bits.

He'd spent three years of his life with Ruby. His mother never abandoned him completely, so his childhood was made up of intermittent placements. After he met Ruby she took him every time.

Shanni had Ruby's grin. She had Ruby's way of greeting life head on. That was the only reason he was reacting to her like he was, he told himself. Because she was like Ruby.

Yeah, right. She wasn't the least bit like Ruby. She was Shanni.

They lapsed into silence. Pierce turned onto the gravel track leading to the farm, and realized that he didn't want this journey to end. Which was weird. He who held his independence as his most important asset had found a short journey with five kids, a pile of supplies and a woman with a wounded wing great.

'So we're setting out tomorrow,' Shanni said, and he thought, okay, they could keep this businesslike.

'Yep.'

'We didn't go today because—'

'Because you need time to recover.'

'I'm supposed to help you, not the other way round.'

'You saved Donald.'

She thought about that. 'So I did,' she said at last. 'There's a silver lining to every cloud. I might be stuck here…'

'You think you're stuck?'

'Of course I do.' She seemed astonished. 'I mean—' She caught herself. 'I mean, you all seem very nice, but I'm an art curator. This is a career blip. I'm here to regroup and then I'm out of here. So if you find someone else, feel free to employ them.'

'Thank you,' he said gravely.

'Only not tomorrow, cos even though I shouldn't come it was my idea to go to the beach and I really, really want to stay in a castle.'

'So do I,' said Donald.

'Me, too,' said Wendy.

And, to a chorus of 'me, toos', he turned into the farm. With his temporary housekeeper. Temporary childminder. Temporary… relationship?

He didn't do relationships. Even temporary ones.

CHAPTER SIX

SHANNI woke at three in the morning. Her shoulder hurt.

Actually, it throbbed.

'Wuss,' she told herself, but her shoulder wasn't in the mood to be told it was making too much fuss.

She needed painkillers. The doctor had given her lethal-looking night-time pills with instructions that she'd need them to go to sleep. But he'd said they'd make her dozy, and she was a bit wary of being dozy in this house. What if there was another bull? She'd taken a couple of milder analgesics and had managed to go to sleep, but now those bright blue suckers she'd put in the kitchen medicine cabinet looked pretty inviting.

The house was in darkness. She was still in the girls' bedroom. Wendy and Abby were fast asleep. Carefully she threw back the covers, winced as the movement hurt her arm, then padded her way downstairs to the kitchen.

Pierce was sitting at the table, a sheath of plans

spread out before him. He looked like a man who'd been working for hours.

He was wearing bright blue pyjamas. He had serious-looking glasses perched low on his nose. He'd been raking his hair with his fingers. His curls had separated into rake marks. He needed a shave again.

He was seriously cute.

He looked up, and she jumped.

'Hey,' he said, sounding as startled as she was. 'It's me who's supposed to jump.'

'Did I scare you?'

'If you're asking whether the sight of five feet three inches of woman with pyjamas covered in pink pigs and with one arm in a sling is enough to terrify me—you could be right.' He stretched, like a big cat, and rose lazily to his feet. 'Your arm's hurting?'

'I… Yes.' Maybe the pink pigs weren't such a good idea, she thought. They'd been a Kris Kringle Christmas gift from the gallery staff. She'd shoved them right to the back of her bureau, but when she'd been packing to come home she'd thought, why not, no one's going to see me in bed ever again.

But she wouldn't have minded a bit of feminine lace right now. Or even plain flannelette. Just not pigs.

'They're great,' Pierce said, and grinned. There it was again—that grin. He could make her heart do somersaults.

She was his temporary housekeeper. And, after

Mike, your selection criteria is seriously flawed, she told herself. *Do not think cute.*

'They're all the fashion in London,' she said defensively.

'I believe you.' His smile widened.

Whoa. *Stop it, stop it, stop it.*

'Sit by the fire,' he told her. He walked round and pulled the fireside rocker forward.

'I'm all right.'

'Sit.' Before she knew what he intended, he caught her round the waist, picked her up and deposited her in the chair. Just as if she was one of his kids.

She didn't feel like one of his kids. She felt imperiled.

There's a dumb thing to think, she told herself crossly. Just because he's so…male.

'I'll make you some cocoa,' he said, turning his back to her, which was a relief. When he wasn't smiling the pressure dropped. Just a bit. 'You shouldn't take those pills on an empty stomach. Cocoa and chocolate cookies coming up. I can strongly recommend the cookies, and there's nothing like a nice hot cup of cocoa to make you sleep.'

'Thank you, grandpa.'

'Hey, we both have pyjamas on,' he retorted. 'If I'm grandpa, you're grandma.'

She should make some smart retort. She should. But the first six retorts she made in her head were all classified dangerous after the very barest of examination. She subsided into what she hoped was dignified silence while he filled the kettle.

'We can go to the beach tomorrow,' he told her. 'I've had no less than five phone calls offering to take care of the cattle any time I need a break. Thanks to you.'

He was smiling at her too warmly. Much too warmly. She was starting to colour.

'What are you working on?' she asked, as much for something to fill the silence as for interest. In truth her shoulder was hurting so much she shouldn't be interested in anything but pain relief. The fact that, despite the pain, she was very interested indeed in a man in blue pyjamas was a bit of a worry.

Actually, it was a very definite worry, and it was growing more definite every second.

'A railway station,' he said. 'Want to see?'

'I… Yes.' She went to rise, but he was before her, hauling the table sideways so it was in reach. He lifted the first set of plans and laid it on her knee. 'This is the overall concept. The rest is detailed working plans.'

He went back to his cocoa making. She tried to turn her attention to the plans.

Which suddenly wasn't difficult. These were…

Amazing.

'This is huge,' she whispered. 'A major metropolitan hub. A whole new network. I think I saw this advertised in London. Didn't they run a competition for ideas?'

'They did. We won.'

'We?'

'My company.'

She whistled. This was almost enough to make her forget her shoulder. She lifted plan after plan, looking at the meticulous detail as well as the truly astounding master plan.

'But you're brilliant,' she whispered at last.

'I know,' he said laying cocoa, chocolate cookies and two blue pills before her. 'And handsome and rugged and strong and heroic, and so humble you wouldn't believe.'

She choked.

'Take your pills,' he ordered.

'Yes, sir.' She did.

'Ruby says you're no halfwit yourself,' he said.

'Ruby says the nicest things.'

'She does, doesn't she? Oh, and speaking of Ruby and her boys…' He turned and rustled under the pile of papers on the table. 'I rang Blake tonight— Blake's another of Ruby's boys—about the dreaded Mike and his use of your shared credit card.'

'Hey.' What was he doing interfering in her life? 'You have no right…'

'I don't,' he said regretfully. 'That's what Blake said. He says maybe Mike acted unlawfully, but he wouldn't know unless you let him have access to your details. He faxed me a permission form for you to fill in. If you want to sign it he'll look into it.'

'There's nothing Blake can do.'

'He's a Ruby's boy,' Pierce said modestly. 'Between us, Ruby says we're going to rule the world. A Ruby dynasty.'

'It's no good establishing dynasties if none of you intend to have families,' she said absently. She ate a chocolate cookie, absently read Blake's form, thought what the heck, filled it in, signed it and went back to considering Pierce. She shouldn't. But he really was well worth considering. 'But maybe you could form a foster dynasty,' she suggested. 'A world run by people without mothers.' She thought about her own and glowered. 'It might just work.'

'Hey,' he said, guessing where her thoughts had gone. 'They only sublet their house.'

'*Only*,' she said darkly. 'I have a doll called Susie Belle I keep in my bedroom. If any kid's messing with Susie Belle…'

'You want us to organise a Susie Belle hit? Armed men, at dead of night, sweeping in, "Nobody move, the doll's ours."'

She grinned. 'You want to try?'

'Sam works for the SAS. We'd put him in charge.'

'Sam, as in Ruby's Sam?'

'I told you—we're a dynasty.'

'So you are.'

She gazed at him, for just a moment too long. Suddenly flustered, she turned away, gazing into the flames through the open fire-door.

Much safer.

She was aware—or she thought she was aware, but there was no way she was checking—that Pierce was looking at her, but she didn't look back. Flames. Right. Concentrate.

'You should go back to bed,' he said, and his voice sounded a bit strained.

She should. But this was great. The room still smelled faintly of the wonderful beef curry Dwayne's mother had appeared with at dinner. Two cakes and the remains of an apple strudel sat on the bench waiting for tomorrow. This was a lovely, warm, food-laden kitchen, with a fantastic fire-stove, and a man working at the kitchen table on plans that were amazing. A really nice man…

'I'll go back to bed as soon as the tablets work,' she said. 'Go back to your plans.'

He did. He focused on his work with absolute attention. After a bit he seemed to forget she was there, which suited her. She could watch him surreptitiously, taking stock.

He really was the strangest mix.

He was about as different from Mike as it was possible for a man to be. Mike would have jumped her by now, she thought. Despite the pigs.

Pierce seemed totally oblivious.

Which was just as well, she thought, if she had to spend the next couple of weeks with him…

She shouldn't go to the beach. He wouldn't need her at the castle.

'I will need you,' he said, and she blinked. He was writing on the side of the plans. His hand didn't pause. How could he know what she was thinking?

'Why will you need me?'

'Because Donald trusts you.'

'Donald?'

'He's a strange kid. He's been watching me for a year now, and yet I don't think he trusts me. He's waiting for me to ditch them or something. He tries to take care of them all himself, and he tries to pretend they don't need me. But in one fell swoop he's figured that you're okay.'

'Clyde was good for something.'

'I guess he was.' He sighed. 'Poor old man.'

'Clyde, you mean?'

'Yeah. He's quiet as a baby tonight. I put him in the girls' paddock. It's a bit early for joining, but I thought a bit of sex might take his mind off his trauma.'

'You worry about them all,' she said softly. 'Even Clyde.'

'Yeah. Some bachelor,' he said grimly, and went back to his drawings.

The pills were kicking in a little. Or maybe it was

the warmth and the cocoa and the company. She felt sleepy and warm, and like she didn't want to move for a hundred years.

'You're not a bachelor,' she said sleepily. 'You're a widower.'

There was a pause. 'So I am,' he said, cautious.

'"Widower" is much sexier than "bachelor".'

'I wouldn't know.'

'It's true,' she said, labouring a point that suddenly felt important. 'A widower is very, very sexy.'

'Widower with five kids?'

'Hmm.' She thought about that. 'It's a hitch,' she said. 'But I'm prepared to overlook it.'

There was a long, drawn out silence. She was watching the flames. They were forming shapes. 'I can see a bull in there,' she said.

'A bull...'

'A sort of bull in the inferno. A little something from Dante. I think I might paint it.'

'What's in those pills?'

'Pardon?'

'Nothing.' He grinned and rose, joining her in the lovely warm haze radiated by the stove. 'Bedtime.'

'I want to stay here.'

'I can see that you do. But I have work to do, and you're distracting me.'

'You're distracting yourself.'

'Thank you,' he said gravely. 'Is your shoulder still hurting?'

'My shoulder's lovely.'

'Then it's bedtime for you, princess,' he said, and he bent and lifted her with the effortless ease he'd used before.

She should take umbrage. She should…

She wound her arms round his neck and held on. 'Nice.'

'So Ruby tells me.'

'Ruby's right. She says you're the nice one. You're certainly the one with the sexiest pyjamas.'

'Have you been on the whisky?'

She thought about that. 'No,' she said at last. 'Should I have? Can we have one?'

'If I give you a whisky you'll be out for the count,' he told her. 'I have a feeling you don't take painkillers too often.'

'Pain?'

'That's what I mean, sweetheart.' He was climbing the stairs. She was cradled against him. He had the nicest pyjamas, she thought hazily. They were made of the same soft fabric as her pink pigs. She put her cheek on his shoulder and it felt really, really soft…

'Do you mind?' he asked in a voice that was none too steady.

'Do I mind what?'

'Not taking any more of those damned pills,' he said. 'I'm having a word with the doctor tomorrow.'

'The doctor was really, really sorry.'

'Was he?'

'Yes, cos he thought the children were yours and he thought you should have got them inoculated. But I told him you were a hero.'

'Thanks.'

'It's true.' They'd reached the girls' bedroom. He pushed the door wide with his foot and strode across to the last bed in the row. The empty bed. Her bed.

'It's a very, very good thing you're not sleeping in Maureen's big bed,' he said, setting her down on the pillows. Then, as she clung, he reached up and carefully unentwined her fingers from behind his neck.

'Why?'

'It just is. Shanni, let me go.'

She let him go. Just.

'Widowers are very, very sexy,' she whispered.

'So are artists in pyjamas with pink pigs.' He smiled, that magic smile that warmed places within her she hadn't realized were cold.

'Goodnight, Shanni,' he said. He placed a finger on her lips.

'Goodnight yourself,' she whispered. She lifted her hand to his finger and held it where it was, trapped against her lips.

'Shanni…'

'Very, very sexy,' she whispered. 'Are you going to kiss me goodnight?'

He nearly didn't. She saw him retreat, just a little. But he couldn't resist. She knew it with the same cosy certainty that said the night was safe, and life was good, and this house was the most splendid house she'd ever stayed in, and this was the most comfortable bed and...

He kissed her. It was meant to be a feather kiss, over before she knew it, but she wasn't interested in a feather kiss. She put her arms around his neck and tugged him close, finding his mouth, kissing him long and languorously and wonderfully. It felt so right—an extension of the warmth and the wonder of the night. He felt...hers. Her man. She held him close and kissed and kissed, and felt him respond as she knew he must...

Pierce...

But he was pulling away. Unlooping her arms. Forcing her back onto the pillows and moving back.

'No,' he said.

'Yes,' she whispered. 'What did I tell you? Sexy as hell.'

He was backing to the door.

'Kiss me again?' she pleaded, and he shook his head. He smiled but his smile was strained.

'You need to sleep.'

'Don't.'

He grinned then. 'Yes you do, princess,' he murmured. She could still see his face. He hadn't turned the light on, so the only light was the moon, but she could see his features. He didn't want to leave as much as she didn't want him to go.

'Pierce?'

His smile faded. 'Goodnight,' he said, and he turned and walked out of the room, closing the door behind him.

CHAPTER SEVEN

THE drive to the castle took three hours, and Shanni blushed the whole way.

Part of the problem was she had too much time to think. She was driving her father's car, unwilling to join the mob in Maureen's wagon and be trapped with no transport at a place she didn't know. Pierce had fretted about her driving with her bad shoulder but she'd ignored him. Her shoulder was better, she'd decreed.

Donald elected to go with her. Pierce was driving Maureen's wagon, and she and Donald followed.

She was never touching those blue pills again.

If the pills had made her act out of character, the least they could do was erase the memory so she didn't know what a fool she'd made of herself the next morning.

Stupid pills.

She'd forced him to kiss her.

And there was the hub of the problem. The kiss was replaying in her head, over and over. Donald was no help. Her small companion hummed a tuneless little ditty over and over, refusing to talk, refusing to help her divert herself.

So she blushed and she gave herself lectures and she blushed again.

She was supposed to be following Pierce, but even seeing the back of his car did her head in. So she fell back, so far that she ended up in Dolphin Bay with Pierce's car nowhere to be seen. She had to stop and ask directions.

The lady at the post office was working on a garish piece of macramé. Macramé followed her everywhere, Shanni thought despondently. What, was there a world resurgence?

But as soon as she asked for directions the postmistress set aside her macramé and beamed.

'How many kiddies this time?'

'Five.'

'Oh, my dear. Oh, you're all going to have a wonderful time. I can't tell you…'

It was a positive note. Shanni returned to the car and headed off again, vaguely worried that Pierce would be worried. She rounded the first bend out of town and there was Pierce, parked in a lay-by. Yes, he was looking worried. But then…

She saw the castle.

She eased off the accelerator and pulled to a stop, astounded.

Donald's small jaw dropped open, and Shanni's jaw dropped in consensus.

'Wow,' said Donald.

'Wow is right,' she whispered.

'It's a real castle,' Donald said.

'I'm scared,' said Shanni.

Donald cast her a doubtful look. 'I don't think it's scary.'

'No?'

'It's just big and pointy, and like Abby's story-books. There probably aren't any ghosts. Abby will like this place.'

What wasn't to like? Shanni thought, stunned. The place seemed straight out of a gothic novel. The castle itself was set high on the cliffs above the sea, with purple-hazed mountains ringing the rear. Built of gleaming white stone, it was all turrets and battlements and vast stone walls. Flags flew from the battlements. Any minute now, she'd see warriors with spears and tubs of hot tar preparing to see them off.

Her car door was tugged open. 'Where the hell have you been?' Pierce demanded, and she jumped about a foot.

'Don't—don't do that.'

'What?'

'You scared me.'

'And you scared me. I was imagining car accidents.'

'Just because I drive sedately when I have children

in the car,' she managed, prim. And then she gazed at the castle again. 'You've seen this before?'

'I helped with the renovations. Isn't it great?'

'I… It's unbelievable. What's a castle doing on the coast of New South Wales?'

'The original Loganaich Castle was in Scotland. It got bombed in the Second Word War. The last earl had been wounded in the war. He'd suffered a gutful of midges and fog and he craved sun, so he rebuilt here. Isn't it fantastic?'

'Fantastic,' she said cautiously. 'As an architect…'

'Oh, I disapprove,' he said, and grinned. 'Talk about an environmental white elephant… But now it's built I'm just as gobsmacked as the next man, and helping with the renovations was great. Talk about preserving kitsch. It's fantastic.' He peered in to Donald. 'What do you reckon, Donald?'

'Shanni says it's scary,' Donald said.

'What's to be scared of? There aren't any dungeons. The old earl thought they could safely be left in Scotland.' He pointed to the highest turret. 'That turret contains the kids' bedrooms. You want to sleep in a turret?'

'With…' Donald gulped. 'With Wendy and everyone?'

'Yes.'

Donald cast an uncertain glance at Shanni. 'And with Shanni?'

'Yes,' Shanni said before Pierce could respond. 'It's an excellent idea of Donald's that I sleep with the kids. Thank you for inviting me, Donald.'

'Still scared?' Pierce teased and grinned, and she knew he wasn't referring to a few ghosts.

'I was on pills last night,' she said with as much dignity as she could muster.

'So you've told me five times today already. You want to come into the castle?'

He had to stop smiling, she thought desperately. He must. She was falling, falling, falling, and here was a crazy medieval castle looming before her, telling her she should leave reality outside and indulge in make-believe.

Yeah, right. Fairy tale or not, she had to keep her feet firmly on the ground.

'Forget last night, and yes please,' she managed.

The owners and the staff of Loganaich Castle were as stunning as the castle itself. Shanni had expected some sort of institution. There'd be kindly staff, she'd thought, efficient but ordered. Here though there seemed to be chaos. It hit from the moment they drove into the castle foregate.

There were three small girls sitting on the front step, twin girls aged about six and a toddler between them. They were concentrating on very large, pink ice-cream cones.

At their feet was a dog. A weird dog. The dog was brown, white and furry, with long floppy ears, a stretched-out body about the size of a cocker spaniel, a tail that added another two feet in length and legs that were about six inches long. The dog was looking at the girls, adoration mixed with the intense concentration of a dog expecting a dropped ice-cream at any minute.

Pierce pulled up first and Shanni pulled up behind. They emerged from the cars, and the three girls on the steps waved their ice-creams. Dangerously.

'Hi,' said one of the two twins. 'Are you Mr MacLachlan?'

'Yes,' said Pierce.

'Susie said there was a daddy but not a mummy,' the other twin said, and she looked at Shanni as if she'd been sold a pup. 'She said the mummy died.'

'I'm Shanni,' Shanni offered. 'I'm the…housekeeper. Is there anyone…?'

'Hello.' As if on cue, a woman came flying out the front door, looking flustered. She was dressed in soil-coated overalls and she was covered in mud. She flew down the steps, beaming, holding out her hands in greeting. 'Pierce. And Ruby's Shanni. Welcome.' Then, as Pierce took an instinctive step back, she looked down at her hands and winced. 'Whoops. I should have washed. Sorry. I've been digging spuds.'

'Spuds?'

'Isn't that right? I'm American, but I'm learning.' She wiped her hands on her overalls, collecting as much mud as she was discarding. 'I'm Susie, Lady of Loganaich. Isn't that a weird title? It makes me think I should be wandering the halls, moaning and clanking chains. Hamish has gone into town for supplies, so I'm the reception committee, but we're having a bit of a disaster with the pumpkin patch. It's too wet and we've rot. Rot this early spells ruin. I'm building it up with pea straw. Jodie's making beds and Kirsty's helping. She shouldn't be, but she's insisting. Which of you has the chicken pox?'

'Bessy,' Pierce said, sounding dazed, motioning into the car where Bessy sat in her baby seat, gazing out with interest. 'She was miserable before the spots came out, but only three spots appeared and now she's cheered up.'

'But you've all had them,' Susie said as the kids started piling out of the car. 'You guys deserve a medal. Did it really itch?'

'It was horrible,' Abby said, tucking in behind Pierce and regarding the muddy Susie with caution.

'Pierce said we were making him itch just to look at us,' Wendy added.

'Well, you guys have come to the right spot here for post-itch therapy,' Susie declared. 'This is the best place in the world for getting rid of any recalcitrant itch. You lie in the surf and soak for hours. You guys ever been to the beach?'

'N…no,' Wendy said, gripping Abby's hand.

'Hardly any kids have seen the beach when they come to us.' A rangy young man dressed in work overalls and bearing a crowbar emerged from a side gate. Susie turned to him and waved. 'Nick, the poxy tribe are here and they've never seen the beach. Shall we show them immediately?' She glanced at the twins and the toddler, who was coated in pink. 'After you've been armed with ice-creams, of course.'

'Excellent,' Nick said, dropping his crowbar. 'Hey, Jodie,' he yelled, up to an open turret window. 'Kirsty. The poxy tribe are here. We're going to the beach.'

'Not without us,' a woman's voice yelled in response from an open window above them.

'Anyone who wants to do something boring like go to the bathroom or tote luggage gets to stay behind and come down with Jodie and Kirsty,' Susie said. 'Kirsty's really pregnant, and she's as slow as a snail. The rest of us… Let's collect our ice-creams and hit the waves.'

Shanni and Pierce were left staring at each other, stunned. The kids, Susie, Nick and Jodie, and Taffy the dog, with a very pregnant Kirsty bringing up the rear, could be heard descending the track to the beach.

'Bessy doesn't go to strangers,' Wendy was explaining to Susie.

'I'm not a stranger,' Susie was saying. 'I'm Susie. I'm Rose's mum. Bessy, you like me, don't you? Nick, are you carrying Rose?'

'Sure,' Nick called from behind. He sounded as American as Susie. 'Me and the twins and Donald are guarding your backs.'

'What's the set-up here?' Shanni asked, dazed, though Pierce looked as dazed as she felt.

'This place is geared up to give kids holidays,' he told her. They were standing in a now deserted castle forecourt. The action was all over the road and down the cliff path.

'But what's its story? Who's Susie? Is she really a…lady?'

'The new Earl of Loganaich—Hamish—was a New York financier before he inherited the castle. Hamish is married to Susie. Hamish's ex-secretary is Jodie. Jodie's husband, Nick, is a social worker they invited to come out from America to help them set this place up. Susie's twin, Kirsty, and her husband are local doctors in Dolphin Bay. The twins are theirs—Susie's nieces. Rose—the toddler—is Susie's.' He grinned. 'Don't look like that. It'll become clearer. I came here to do renovation plans, and for the opening, but I'm still trying to match dogs and kids to grown ups. It's chaos, but it's great chaos.'

'It looks fabulous. And you never thought of bringing the kids here before?'

'To be honest, I've been too busy to think past the nose on my face since Maureen arrived,' he confessed. 'It wasn't until you suggested we all go to the beach that I thought of it.' He hesitated and then admitted, 'Yeah, and Ruby's known here. Even if I had thought of it I'd have worried it'd get back to her. Me not coping with five kids.'

'You don't mind her knowing now?'

'Susie swears it can stay in confidence.'

'And Susie's fine with the chicken pox?'

'There aren't any other kids here at the moment. They keep two weeks of every six open for emergencies, and we slotted into that. Everyone here has either been poxed or inoculated.'

'So.' She swallowed. More than ever she thought she wasn't needed. She'd wanted time at the beach, but this was starting to seem…dangerous. Where was the excuse to stay? 'I should just slope off.'

'Why?'

'I'm hardly needed.' The kids had reached the beach now. Their astonished cries could be heard from where they stood. '*You're* hardly needed, and I'm needed even less. The kids have disappeared without a backward glance.'

'I'll be doing some work here. As per your suggestion.'

'By the look of it you'll be able to. Even Bessy's gone with them. So I can just…go.'

But the whoops and cries from the beach were enticing. She wanted to walk over to the edge of the cliff and look.

'To Ruby's?' Pierce asked. 'To the macramé?'

'I can find somewhere. I'm not exactly friendless.'

'I'm sure you're not.' He hesitated, looking across the road as well. The kids' voices floated up, delirious with excitement. 'We need to go and see…'

'*You* need to go and see.'

'We both need,' he said, suddenly decisive. 'You've just promised you'll sleep in the kids' wing, and I don't see you breaking that promise.' He put his hands on her forearms, fixing her to the spot. 'Shanni, you suggested this. This was your idea, and it's a fantastic one. I employed you to look after my kids and you're doing just that in bringing them here. You've had a rotten time in London—anyone can see that. You've also been a lot sicker with your influenza than these kids have been with their chicken pox.'

'How do you know?'

'You're washed out.'

'I am not!'

'And you have bigger shadows under your eyes than I do. The accommodation here is booked for two adults and five children. I intend to play with the kids and do some work. I think you should spend the next two weeks lying on the beach getting your colour back.'

'I am *not* washed out.'

'So you normally look like Susie's moaning and clanking Lady of the Castle?'

'I...' She floundered, wishing for a mirror. Or an exit. 'I don't. I'm sure I don't.'

He grinned. 'You're sure you normally don't look as pale and wan as this? That's what I thought. You've two weeks at the beach. Get used to it. Now... You don't happen to remember what case we packed our swimming gear in?'

'The red one.'

'There you go, then. You're useful already. Let's go join the troops. Oh, and Shanni...'

'What?' she said, trying to figure whether she was being railroaded against her wishes or whether she really did want to stay.

He placed his finger on her lips. The movement was so unexpected she took a step back.

'The kiss last night,' he said, and he was smiling. 'I'm not taking it seriously, so neither should you.'

She shouldn't be here.

Shanni lay in the dark in her fabulous bedroom and stared at the moonlit ceiling, wondering what on earth she was doing, staying in a castle for disadvantaged children.

Things had moved so fast in the last few weeks she felt...weird. One moment she was running a struggling but hip art gallery in London, the next she was recuperating from flu in a castle on the coast of New South Wales. She had a velvet canopy over her bed. She was surrounded by gold embossed wallpaper. There was a fireplace at the end of the room so big and so ornate it looked like a work of art in its own right. The bathroom down the end of the hall had a picture of Queen Victoria staring sternly down at her, a chandelier hung from the ceiling and an aspidistra dangled over the cistern.

She'd giggled when she'd seen the picture first, but when she'd gone back later Queen Vic's matriarchal stare had seemed disapproving.

'I'll make a donation and pay my keep,' she'd told the monarch, but Victoria's disapproval had only seemed to deepen.

She *could* go and stay with Ruby. She was sure Pierce would sign Ruby's dratted consent form.

Or she could camp on Jules's floor.

But for how long?

And suddenly it all seemed overwhelming. Grey and heavy and hard.

It had all happened too fast. Finding Mike and his horrible floozy had been dramatic and sordid, and she'd been too ill with influenza to think straight. But strangely now, in this fabulous bedroom, with five needy kids within calling distance, with Pierce just down the hall, it was the first time she'd seen clearly the mess her life was in.

She was twenty-eight years old—twenty-nine in three weeks. She'd lost her gallery and her apartment. She had no money and no career.

'And no one will employ me,' she whispered. 'I'm qualified as a curator of an art gallery, yet the only one I've ever owned went bust. Some qualification. I'll never get another job as a curator and I know it.

'Maybe a provincial gallery...

'It's too small a world. Mike will have bad-mouthed me, and he has powerful friends. I lost my head and my career's kaput.'

She sniffed.

'Don't you dare cry,' she told herself. 'Not'

'Shanni?'

It was a child's voice. Hauled out of the indulgence of a good sob, Shanni made do with a bigger sniff and sat up in bed. She reached for the bedside lamp. Or should she make that the bedside *chandelier*? There was more crystal here than in the royal Palace of Versailles. Imitation crystal, she told herself. Susie had given them a grand tour, giggling at the ostentatious furnishings. 'Deidre thought it was a hoot, making this place as kitsch as she could. Don't you just love Ernst and Eric?'

Ernst and Eric were the two suits of armour guarding the stairs. Made in Japan.

'Ersnt and Eric are the Loganaich keepers of secrets,' Susie had told them, deeply earnest as she introduced the children to the suits. 'Anything you say to these guys, they'll take it to the grave.'

But right now Wendy seemed to want a warmer audience than two tin warriors. 'Shanni, are you asleep?' Her voice was trembling.

'Nope,' Shanni said, sniffing again and trying to sound cheerful. 'I'm sitting in my royal bed waiting for a few minions to cater to my every whim. And my whim is that you talk to me.' As Wendy ventured tentatively into the room, Shanni tossed back her covers and moved to one side. 'Come on in. It's warm in here.'

Wendy didn't need two invitations. She practically bolted over to the bed, dived in and pulled the covers to her chin.

'Hey,' Shanni said, startled. 'You're not scared of ghosts, are you?'

'N...no.'

'Well, what?'

'I had...a dream. I thought it was real.'

She was trembling all over. Shanni's self-absorption disappeared in an instant.

She should have slept with the girls tonight, she thought, but Wendy and Abby had chosen a room just above her head, a turret with two bower windows and a bed in each bower. The girls had taken one look and whooped with joy, and there was only room for two. The boys had a similar room on the other side of the turret. Shanni's and Pierce's bedrooms were right underneath, so they could hear anyone call. Pierce had Bessy in a crib in his room and Shanni was in solitary splendour.

But it had felt wrong, Shanni thought as she hugged the little girl close. Why? What was she thinking? That she ought to be closer to these kids?

'Problem?'

She glanced up and Pierce was in the doorway. He was still in jeans and pullover.

What was he doing, wandering the castle at night, still dressed at this hour? He must be tuned to the kids with extrasensory perception, she thought, to have heard Wendy's soft call.

'Wendy's here,' she said.

'Wendy…'

Wendy was about as close to Shanni as it was possible to get, huddled under the bedclothes, her whole body shaking.

'Nightmares,' Shanni said, and Pierce winced.

'Again.' He took a couple of steps into the room and Wendy shrank tighter against Shanni.

'No…'

Pierce stopped as if struck. 'Hell, Wendy.'

'Don't swear,' Shanni said automatically. 'Hey, Wendy it's only Pierce.'

The child was shaking so much Shanni was starting to be seriously worried.

'Go away,' Wendy whispered. 'I don't need...'

'She's had these nightmares before,' Pierce said, staying where he was. 'They're awful, but she never lets me near. I took her to a child psychologist but she won't talk about them.'

'Nightmares are ghastly,' Shanni said.

'I know.' Pierce looked lost, Shanni thought. And suddenly, she thought, he *did* know. This man had had his nightmares, too. Was he still having them?

'What was your nightmare about?' she asked Wendy, hugging her close.

A fierce shake of her head was the only response.

'I used to have nightmares about frogs.' Shanni grimaced. 'Great, big slimy frogs. Frogs taking over the world. Horrid.'

'Frogs are cute,' Wendy whispered.

'Not my frogs.'

Silence.

'And I bet you had nightmares too,' she said to Pierce. 'What were your nightmares about?'

The silence lengthened.

'I don't...' he said at last, and Shanni sighed.

'So if we sent you to a child psychologist you wouldn't tell us yours either?'

'This is Wendy we're talking about.'

'It is.' She hugged the little girl so tight she felt their ribs collide. Wendy was too thin. A waif.

'Wendy, we need to talk about this,' Pierce said

heavily. 'I know you're scared. I know the dark seems awfully lonely.' He hesitated. 'Once upon a time I felt like that.'

'Maybe sometimes you still do,' Shanni whispered. 'Sometimes we all do.'

'No.'

'Grown ups are sometimes scared, too,' she told Wendy. 'The thing to do is to talk about it. Honest. I talked to my mum after my frog nightmares, and she took me to the zoo and we learned all about frogs. We learned that the world's biggest frog is the Goliath, and it's bigger than my dad's foot. Which is pretty huge. But it still only eats insects. Mum took me to a pond on our friend's farm and we collected frog eggs. Dad dug a pond in the garden and we filled it with all the things frogs love. The eggs hatched into tadpoles and the tadpoles turned into frogs. I called them names like Hoppit and Cassidy. So then I started dreaming about real frogs, and my nightmares just…stopped.'

'Your parents loved you,' Pierce said softly.

'They abandoned Susie Belle,' Shanni retorted. 'My beautiful doll,' she explained to Wendy. 'Let's not be too nice about my parents. Wendy, what are your nightmares about?'

'I want…'

'What do you want?'

'Pierce to go away,' Wendy whispered.

The words were so shocking that Shanni froze. She glanced up at Pierce, and she saw something on his face that shocked her further. Pain. Pure, unadulterated pain.

Whatever was happening here, it wasn't Pierce Wendy was afraid of, she thought. That look…

'Pierce is our friend,' she whispered. 'Pierce loves you.'

'He's…'

'What are the nightmares?' she pressed.

'Dark,' Wendy murmured.

But it was too much. Pierce was backing out the door. He looked stricken.

'I'll leave you,' he said, woodenly, stiffly. 'I'll be up on the battlements. Too far away to hear.'

Shanni wanted to call him back, but she knew she mustn't. Wendy was still pressed tight against her. Was she fully awake from the nightmare, or were traces of it still lingering?

Was Wendy afraid of Pierce?

This didn't make sense. Wendy seemed desperate for this oddly constructed family to work. She must have had plenty of opportunities with the social welfare people to say Pierce wasn't treating her well, that she wanted to leave.

Or…abuse? That didn't bear thinking of, but Shanni took a deep breath, swallowed and decided she had to be an adult here. She needed to wipe any preconceived ideas out of her head and tackle this like she knew nothing. Which she did.

'Pierce is gone,' she said.

'I know.'

'So you can tell me what the nightmares are now.'

'I… No.'

'Wendy, I saved Donald from the bull,' she said, deciding a bit of bossiness was in order. 'I'll save you from your terrors, too, but I need to know what they are.'

There was a long silence. Then, 'Dark,' Wendy whispered.

'Dark?'

'I… Yes.'

'There's a night light in your room. Isn't it light enough for you?'

'Just… When I go to sleep…'

'It's dark when you go to sleep?'

'The cupboard,' Wendy said, and Shanni held her breath.

'What cupboard?'

'He puts me in it. He hates me, cos if he hits the kids I tell Mum. Mum's in bed—she's always sick. And every time…'

'Is this Pierce?' Shanni interrupted, appalled. The nightmare obviously was mixing past with present, horrifically.

'No.' It was barely a whisper. 'The other…'

'Another man?'

'We were with him for ages. Mum said we had to stay with him cos she didn't have anywhere else to go. So I didn't tell her about the cupboard. I'd tell her if he hit the kids, but she got upset when I told her anything. I told the kids it was okay. I didn't mind. I pretended it was a—a game. But it wasn't. Then one night he hit Donald, really hard. He made Donald's eye swell up and I kicked him, even harder than he hit Donald. But then he locked us both up. Only, Donald cried so loud that Abby went and told Mum. Mum got up and yelled and yelled, and Donald said I was always in the cupboard. Even when I told him not to say it. Then Mum cried all night. The next day, Mum put us all in the car and we went to Pierce's.'

Dear God.

I'm not qualified to deal with this, Shanni thought desperately. I don't know what to do.

But she was all Wendy had. Apart from Pierce, who Wendy was obviously mixing in her head with her mother's ghastly partner. Only in her sleep, she thought, but it was enough to mean Pierce couldn't help her now.

'Wendy, that's a dreadful story,' she said. 'It's awful. How dare he treat you like that.'

'I...'

'He ought to be arrested.' She was angry, and she

decided it couldn't hurt to let her anger show. 'Of all the ghastly, scary things… Oh, Wendy, how could you bear it? And you had to look after the other children, too.'

'It was…dark.'

'And your mother didn't know?'

'Once I tried to tell her, but she got so upset she got out of bed and fell over. He told her I'd been naughty, and he said he'd only put me in there for a minute. But it was for hours and hours. And it was over and over again. All night, sometimes. Until Donald, I tried not to say.'

'Oh, Wendy, love,' Shanni whispered. 'Oh, my brave Wendy. You're the bravest kid I know. Bar none.'

'I hate the nightmares,' she said.

'You know Pierce isn't like this man.'

'I… I know.'

Shanni took a deep breath, then swung her legs out of bed, got up and turned on the overhead light. This suddenly seemed of immense importance.

'You know I saved Donald from the bull.'

Wendy nodded, not sure where Shanni was going.

'Wendy, I swear to you, if anyone else were to hurt you I'd react exactly the same as if they were the bull. No matter who. Do you believe that?' She put her hand under the little girl's chin and forced her to meet her eyes. 'Wendy, you have to believe it.'

'I… I do.'

'So, are you afraid of Pierce?'

She was holding her breath. Surely she couldn't be wrong about Pierce's character, she thought, but this child was trusting her, and suddenly Shanni knew the enormity of what was being offered. Trust…

'Please,' she whispered under her breath, but she forced her face to stay absolutely clear, absolutely empty, non-judgemental, not likely to react to the worst…

'No,' Wendy whispered.

'You didn't want him to come in just now.'

'No, I…'

'You what?'

'It's just the dreams,' Wendy said desperately. 'Our mum said Pierce was a friend. She said we could trust him for ever. She said we'd be safe. And we are, and he's nice as nice, and sometimes I even hug him like the other kids, but at night I have dreams and he gets all mixed up with…with the other one.'

'Has Pierce ever done anything to you in a way you don't like? Anything at all?' Was this Shanni asking these sort of questions? She was a city girl with no responsibilities, with her head in the art world. What was she doing, asking questions like these?

But she must.

'No,' Wendy said, and there was something about her that told Shanni she couldn't lie about this. It was too important. For some reason she'd decided to admit Shanni to her confidence, and she was going as far as she could.

'So there's no reason to be afraid of him except the dreams?'

'I can't stop dreaming,' Wendy said desperately. 'I try and I try, but the dark comes.'

'Oh, sweetheart,' Shanni said, trying not to cry. 'You're safe now. You're absolutely safe. I'm protecting you. Pierce is protecting you. So is everyone in this castle, and tomorrow we're going for a swim at the beach before breakfast.'

'I… I know.'

'Who cut your hair?' Shanni asked suddenly. The child's crop looked as if it had been attacked by a pruning saw. Ragged and uneven, it ranged from almost touching the collar of her pyjamas to being almost scalp-short.

'I did,' Wendy said, distracted from nightmares for a moment. 'When we had the chicken pox. Abby spilled her drink, and I was mopping it up under the table when Donald spilled craft glue. It went into my hair. I tried to wash it out but it wouldn't wash. So I cut it.'

'What did Pierce say when he saw?'

'He phoned the hairdresser, but she wouldn't cut it cos of the chicken pox.' She put a hand through her ragged curls. 'It's okay.'

'It's not,' Shanni said. Here at last was something she could do. Girl stuff. 'After your swim tomorrow, what say you and me go into town and find a hair-dresser? And a clothes shop. You're wearing the same clothes as Abby.'

'Mum said it was easier.'

'Yes, but your mum was sick, and I like a challenge.' She grinned. 'There's nothing like a bit of retail therapy to drive away nightmares. I'll hit Pierce for an advance on my wages if he won't pay.'

'Retail therapy?'

'Clothes,' Shanni said. 'Clothes and shoes and hair. Pretty stuff. Girl stuff. You're eleven years old, Wendy MacLachlan. You can be a kid and have fun all you want to, but it's time you had a play at being a young lady.'

CHAPTER EIGHT

PIERCE stood on the battlements and stared out over the moonlit sea. This was one of the most beautiful places on earth. He should be soaking in the beauty of the night.

Instead, all he could think of was the haunted face of the child he'd just left. Shadows. So many shadows, haunting them all. How the hell could he face them down for Wendy when he hadn't faced down his own?

'She's asleep.' The soft words made him turn. Shanni had come up beside him, so close she was touching him. She was wrapped in a blanket, her pyjamas underneath.

The pig pyjamas?

'I was going to leave her in bed with me, but she wanted Abby. So I took her back to bed and waited till she was asleep.' She hesitated. 'Great view,' she said at last.

'Yes.'

'She's quite a kid.'

'I know that.'

'Did you know she's been abused?'

He stilled. The night seemed to freeze. 'Abused…'

'Not sexually,' Shanni said. 'Not that I can figure. But the last of Maureen's partners seems to have knocked her round. She's been locked in wardrobes in the dark.'

'I guessed something like that,' he said heavily.

'You guessed?'

'I took the kids to a psychologist just after Maureen died. They were all traumatized to some extent—well, they would be when their mother just died—but the way Wendy flinched if I raised my voice… But Wendy wouldn't talk to the psychologist. There was nothing I could do to make her.'

'It's some commitment you've taken on.'

'I never meant to,' he said heavily, and dug his hands deep into his pockets. 'God knows I wanted nothing to do with all this.'

'Then why did you take them on?'

'I thought it'd be easy,' he said explosively. 'They were almost totally self-contained. Before Maureen died I was allowed to do nothing. Wendy and Bryce controlled Donald and Abby. They kept out of my way. They were quiet—unnaturally quiet, but I didn't know that. I'm thinking now that Maureen must have ordered them to leave me alone—to let me do nothing for them. Anyway, it was only after Bessy was born—

after I'd made my promise and my commitment—
that I started seeing the chasm I'd jumped into.'

'Chasm?'

'I was supposed to hire a housekeeper and head
back to the city,' he snapped. 'How easy's that? I'd
come down at weekends when I could, pat them on
the head, feel good about keeping them all together
and then leave again.'

'Only now you see that they desperately need
someone more than a housekeeper?'

'I can't give that sort of commitment.'

'I think you already have.'

'I haven't.'

'You're their adoptive father. There's no one else.'

'Hell, Shanni, I don't do commitment.'

'Because?'

'Look, relationships… They're a disaster.'

'Why?'

'It's none of your business.'

'No.' But… 'Ruby had you four different times when
you were a kid,' she said cautiously. Sure, this was none
of her business, but then when had 'not being her
business' ever stopped her from sticking in her oar? She
was too far in now to draw back. She had obligations
to Wendy, and if that meant facing down Pierce's
ghosts then so be it. Shanni, family counsellor. *Right.*

'So that meant you kept going back to your
mother?' she asked.

For a moment she thought he wasn't going to answer. Then he shrugged.

'Whenever she had a relationship.'

'So when she had a man, she wanted you as well? How did that work?'

'She played happy families. My mother loved talking about "my husband". "My son". Only she had to have them both. Both or nothing. So, when the relationship ended, back I'd go to foster homes. To Ruby when I was lucky.'

'So the end of each relationship meant you went back to being safe with Ruby.' She whistled. 'Boy, a psychiatrist could have a carnival with you.'

'Do you mind?' he demanded, and she shrugged and managed a smile.

'No, cos I'm interested.' She hugged her blanket closer. 'And I've just played psychologist with Wendy, so I might as well do it with you. Does this all mean you'll never want marriage or your own kids—which is why you offered to take on Maureen's? Maybe you even thought it could protect you even more from relationships.'

His face was frozen, blank and hard. 'I'm going to bed.'

'Did anyone lock you in a cupboard?'

There was a loaded silence. She'd gone too far, she thought. Whoops. Was she doing more harm than good? That was starting to be the story of her life.

'You did get the sort of treatment that was meted out to Wendy,' she said softly. 'You and Maureen both. Which is why you had to help her. Oh, Pierce.'

'This is crazy.' He was staring out to sea, carefully not looking at her. He was big and tough and carefully self-contained—rigidly self-contained. 'I will not have anyone feeling sorry for me.'

'No, why would you?' she whispered. 'You're a wealthy bachelor with a brilliant professional reputation and the world at your feet. As opposed to me, a penniless practically orphan.'

'Orphan?'

'They changed the locks on my childhood home.'

'You're how old?'

'They've locked me out from Susie Belle.'

He choked. His laughter made her smile. That was what she'd been aiming for. 'It's not such a tragedy,' she admitted softly. 'As you imply, I'm a big girl. I'll deal with my trauma myself.' Her smile faded. 'But Wendy can't.'

'I'll talk to Nick tomorrow. He's a qualified child psychologist, and he's worked with damaged kids.'

'This castle has everything,' Shanni said and went back to looking out to sea. She was too close to Pierce, she thought, but she couldn't step away without seeming… Without seeming…

'I'd like to take Wendy shopping tomorrow,' she said.

He blinked. He looked confused, she thought. Well, why not? That made two of them.

'Why do you want to go shopping?'

'Retail therapy.' She hesitated. 'I'm thinking this is a glorious time to give these kids the individual attention they crave. They've been a solid bunch until now—they've had to be. But they also need to learn to be their own people.'

'That'll happen soon enough.'

'Sorry? You think learning to be your own person means learning not to need?'

'Doesn't it?'

'Hey, I'm not the psychologist. Ask Nick.'

'I don't need…'

'To ask Nick anything. No. You stand alone. Only, you're not able to. Not now you've officially adopted these kids as yours. If you're not careful, you'll end up needing them as much as they need you.'

'I don't know what you mean.'

'Says the man who walks alone.' She grinned. 'Even Tarzan had his Jane.'

'You're being silly.'

'And you're being serious.' She gazed deliberately out at the sea some more, trying to build some emotional distance between them. 'You know this is the most fantastic place…'

'It is.'

'So why aren't you working?'

'I have been working. I was out in the hall when I heard Wendy. Then I came up here to think.'

'Am I stopping you thinking?'

'Yes.'

'There's a blunt answer,' she said, and chuckled. 'Someone sensitive might take that to mean "shove off".'

'But you're not sensitive?'

'Nope.'

'You should be in bed. You hardly slept last night. I'm sorry Wendy woke you.'

'I'm not. It's far more important to banish demons than sleep. You, as a Tarzan lookalike, should surely know that.'

'Shanni…'

'I know. I'm out of line.' She stared out at the moonlit sea some more. It was almost getting boring, but otherwise she had to look at him, and looking at Pierce was really, really hard. 'You and the kids are so needful.'

'Will you cut it out?'

'I'm not very good at butting out of what's not my business.' She shrugged and then smiled again. 'Besides, it's keeping my mind off my own troubles—and you are paying me for it.'

'Paying you for what?'

'For taking care of the children.'

'So take care of the children,' he snapped, sounding exasperated. 'Leave me out of it.'

'But you guys are all mixed up. You're a family that's not working.'

'We are not a family.' It was practically a roar, and she blinked and took a step back.

'Whoa.'

'I never meant…'

'You never meant you're *not* a family?'

'Yes. No. Hell, Shanni.'

'You're terrified.'

'I'm not. The kids will recover here. I'll get the bulk of my work done. Then we'll set our minds to find a proper housekeeper.'

'It can't work.'

'Why not?'

'Because you're involved.'

'I'm not involved.'

She paused, not sure where to go from here. This man was all macho male on the outside, but inside she was starting to see he was the same battered kid she'd met almost twenty years ago.

'Hey, the human race isn't scary,' she whispered.

'Isn't it?'

'No, it's not,' she said, and suddenly she reached out and took his hands. It was a gesture made almost before she knew what she was doing, but it felt right. His hands felt good in hers—big and warm and reassuring.

She was reassuring *him*, she thought, getting a bit confused. It was Pierce who was standing on the battlements looking like he was seeing ghosts. She wasn't taking warmth—she was giving it.

Her blanket had fallen off.

'It's okay to fall for the kids,' she said. 'Love's not really scary.'

'Says the lady with the ice bucket.'

She chuckled. 'See, if I hadn't thought I'd fallen in love, I'd never have known what it was like to toss a bucket of ice water over a naked slimeball and his floozy.'

'And that's a plus?'

'Definitely a plus.'

'You're nuts.'

'I know,' she said, gathering her dignity about her as best she could—slightly tricky when she was covered in pink pigs and her blanket was around her ankles. 'But at least I'm not scared to have a go.'

'At falling in love?'

'At life,' she said with dignity.

'You're saying I'm scared of life?'

'Who knows?' She stared up at him for a long moment. His face looked harsh in the moonlight, dark and angular and stern. But she knew what it was like when he smiled. She wanted him to smile again. Badly.

'Come shopping with Wendy and me in the morning,' she said. She was still holding his hands. For some reason, it seemed almost impossible to let them go.

'I'm not sure what the set-up here is. Hamish and Susie may have plans.'

'They do have plans. Their plans are to give the kids the best time they know how. If that involves us absconding with one small girl to make her happy…'

'The others might get upset.'

'Don't you believe it. They look after each other, this lot, and if we explain Wendy needs some TLC I'll bet they won't make a single protest.'

'TLC?'

'What you need,' she said. 'Tender loving care.'

'Shanni…' He pulled back with his hands, but she didn't let go.

'Stop looking terrified.'

'I am not terrified.'

'Are too.'

'Let go.'

'Of course I will,' she said, and her stupid wayward mouth kept on working even though a lesser mortal—or a more sensible one—would have pulled back long since. 'I'm battered, too, remember? No way am I sliding into another dumb relationship, so you're safe with me. But you're not safe from everyone, Pierce. You can't stay in isolation for ever. It doesn't even feel good.'

'I don't…'

'You don't know what it is to connect.' She smiled, teasing, not sure that what she was doing was sensible or even possible. 'It's great. Just close your eyes and jump.'

And before he could say a word—before he could make a move to protect himself—she released his hands, she placed her own hands on the sides of his face and tugged him down. And she kissed him.

It was meant to be fun. It was meant to be different from the night before—a teasing, bantering kiss, a reminder to this aloof man that connecting could be fun. Maybe after last night she was crazy to make such a gesture. But she did, rightly or not. And what followed…

Her blanket had already fallen off, but now…more than her blanket fell off. Her prudence, her sanity, her dignity, all disintegrated in that tiny instant when his lips came in contact with hers.

It was crazy. It was ridiculous. Unlike last night, this time she'd meant to be a woman in control of the situation, teasing him a little, flirting, maybe even mocking.

But it wasn't working. Because none of those descriptions of what she was doing fitted the reality of now.

She wasn't teasing. Nor was she in control.

She was aware of one thing only. The feel of his lips on hers.

Wow.

As simple as that. *Wow.*

She'd kissed before—of course she'd kissed

before—but where had this feeling been then? This sensation of heat—of fusing—of two halves coming together, connecting as if they'd been torn apart and had been trying to find their way together long since.

Heat...

The sensation of his lips touching hers sent fire right through her. She could feel it coursing from her toes to her fingertips.

What was happening?

This was no longer a fleeting kiss. He was holding her as if, like her, he was no longer cool and controlled, but rather he'd been taken over by a surge of feelings so strong that he could do nothing but give in to them.

How long they stayed like that, she could never afterwards remember. She had bare feet. They were cold against the stones and afterwards in the privacy of her bedroom she would feel them and think she'd been dumb to stay on the battlements for so long.

But that was for later. That was for a time when she could feel her feet. Which wasn't now.

Now.

Her mouth opened under his, and it was like she was melting into him. Pierce...

His kiss deepened and deepened again. She was holding him tight, glorying in the strength of him, the arrant maleness, the sheer wonder of his body against hers.

The fusing of their mouths was no longer enough. He was exploring her body with his hands, holding her close, forcing her breasts to mould against his chest. He was glorying in the sensation of two bodies merging just as much as she was.

An image crept into her mind. How strange, that it should have stayed with her, and resurrected itself here at this time. It was the vision of Pierce as she'd first seen him. Fifteen years old, tall, dark and malnourished, all angular bones and shadows.

The image was so strong that it was almost a part of her. Had she held him in her heart all this time?

It was ridiculous. But it wasn't. It suddenly felt right. The coming together of something that was almost meant to be.

Crazy. Fanciful. But powerful beyond belief, so powerful that it almost terrified her. But it didn't terrify her so much that she pulled away. She couldn't. For along with the terror came something else, something so sweet and so strong that she felt she was changing, a chrysalis shedding its outer shell to reveal a beauty that made her gasp.

Pierce…

She held him close, aware that part of her was kissing that bereft, solitary fifteen-year-old, seeking to comfort, seeking to warm, but most of her was kissing the man he'd become. The man who'd taken in these children when the last thing he wanted was family responsibility. The man who'd driven a bull from her path. The man whose smile made her heart turn over, and whom she wanted with every fibre of her being.

In another time, another place, they might have been so out of control that things might have moved to their logical conclusion. For Shanni there was no question. This kiss had changed her world, and her fragile web of control was so shattered that she could only savour the kiss, savour the feel of him and hold him, never wanting to release him.

Only of course this wasn't another time or another place. They were on the battlements of a children's home. In the building behind them were five children in their charge.

This craziness—this wonder—must be interrupted, and it was. A door opened somewhere beneath them and sensor lights flooded the battlements, like searchlights, blasting into their cocoon of privacy, leaving them exposed and confused. Leaving Shanni...bereft?

'Hey!' It was a woman's voice, yelling from below.

They pulled apart, like guilty teenagers. Shanni's blanket was around her toes. Dazed and dishevelled, fighting to regain some semblance of reality, she bent to retrieve it, leaving Pierce to talk to whoever was calling up to them from below.

'Is that you, Pierce?' It was Susie, Lady of Loganaich.

'Hi,' Pierce called, and his voice sounded as shaken as Shanni was feeling. Maybe even more.

'I should have told you. We've got an alarm wired to sound if people are up there,' Susie said apologetically. 'For the kids.'

Oh heck, Shanni thought dumbly, and did a furtive search for security cameras.

'We're really sorry we woke you,' Pierce called, and Shanni thought, thank God, he could talk, because she didn't think she could.

'You didn't wake me,' Susie called. 'I was pacing the kitchen, thinking wishful thoughts about dill pickles.'

Dill pickles. Okay. There was something really grounding in dill pickles. 'You're pregnant?' Shanni said cautiously, peering over the edge.

'Oh, it's Shanni too,' Susie called cheerfully. 'Hi, Shanni. Yep, I'm just a little bit pregnant.'

'Susie?' A deep male voice called from inside the open castle doors. 'Where the hell are you?'

'I'm out here protecting the battlements,' Susie called, and then as Hamish, Lord of Loganaich, emerged from the big front doors she walked forward and hugged her husband. She did it naturally and easily, as if it was her right. A woman with her man…

Shanni swallowed. The sight was suddenly almost overwhelmingly enticing. This man and this woman loved each other.

Pierce was so close…

'Who's on the battlements?' Hamish growled, kissing his wife tenderly on the top of her head, and then turning to gaze upwards, shielding his eyes from the glare of the floodlights. Shanni and Pierce were lit like Christmas candles. Or like gargoyles decorating the turrets.

Shanni stared at Pierce. He looked ruffled. He looked wonderful. Her Pierce. And suddenly she chuckled, surprising even herself.

'What's funny?' Pierce demanded.

'I was just thinking we made great gargoyles,' Shanni said, loud enough for the couple below to hear. 'Me and my blanket.'

'Speak for yourself,' Pierce growled.

'Mrs and Mr Gargoyle,' she said, deciding humour was the only way to go.

'You didn't look like you were carved in stone when I first saw you,' Susie called up to them.

'Shanni's a bit cuddly for a gargoyle,' Pierce retorted.

The night was spinning out of control again. 'Cuddly?' Shanni demanded, still trying desperately to use humour to defuse the way she was feeling. 'Cuddly?' She'd meant to lose a few pounds...but cuddly?

Pierce was grinning. 'Definitely cuddly.'

She glowered.

'I guess gargoyles play at night,' Susie called. 'When everyone else is in bed.'

'Which is where we should all be right now,' Hamish interjected. He was wearing pyjama bottoms and nothing else. Pierce was the only one among them decorously dressed. 'Are you guys all right?'

'We're fine,' Pierce called back.

'And the kids?'

'Asleep. We were just...talking about the kids.'

'That's what it looked like,' Susie said, and grinned.

'So why are *you* up?' Hamish demanded, turning on his wife again.

'I was looking for a dill pickle.'

'Dill pickle.'

'Why don't we have dill pickles in the larder? Or sardines. Sardines in a can. I can't find them anywhere.'

'This is going to be a very long pregnancy,' Hamish said, sounding resigned. 'You want me to wake up the Dolphin Bay grocer and get a priority delivery of pickles?'

'I can live without them,' Susie said, and sighed. 'If I must. If I can get them very early in the morning.'

'I'd like to go into town tomorrow and get Wendy a haircut,' Shanni called, trying valiantly to get a handle on a conversation that seemed to be getting away from all of them. Especially her. 'I can get dill pickles then.'

'I'll come with you,' Susie said.

'Hey, I'm coming, too,' Pierce said, and the conversation spiralled again.

Why had he said it? Shanni looked at him and then looked away. He seemed more confused than she was.

'We could all go,' Hamish said.

'No.' At least the Lady of Loganaich sounded decisive. 'You can't. Actually, I can't either, cos we promised the rest of the kids they could spend the whole day on the beach, and they don't know how to swim. Imagine that! What a pleasure, to teach them how much fun the water is. And I've suddenly thought—there's anchovy paste in the larder. I think that'll do.'

'God help us,' said Hamish.

'We're wasting time,' Susie retorted. 'I could be spreading toast with anchovy paste this very minute. Goodnight, guys.' And she towed her husband anchovy-wards without another word.

Leaving Shanni with Pierce. Alone.

Really alone.

As soon as the pair below went inside the floodlights flicked off. Hamish and Susie had obviously decided the pair on the roof needed darkness as well as solitude.

This wasn't altogether wise. It wasn't wise at all. Pierce was looking blank. Verging on appalled.

Wrong look. Shanni took a couple of steps backwards.

'There's no need for you to come into town tomorrow,' she managed. 'Wendy and I will be fine.'

'She flinches when I'm near.'

'Only when she forgets…that you're you.'

'So maybe I should be working on that.'

'It's not so important if you're going to step back,' she said diffidently, trying hard not to think how close he was. How she wanted him so much to take her hands again. To…

No. 'If you're really planning on finding a housekeeper and seeing them only on weekends…' she managed.

'It's the sensible thing to do.'

'Is it?'

'I don't commit,' he said, sounding confounded, and she nodded. Okay. A girl had some pride.

'Me either. Not after Mike.'

It was just as well to get that out in the open. It was a declaration that what had just passed between them was an aberration, nothing more.

'I'm sorry I kissed you,' Pierce said, which proved he was following her train of thought and agreeing.

'It was a very nice kiss,' she said cautiously, trying really hard to keep her voice neutral. 'I've never been kissed on battlements before. Though, I thought it was me kissing you.'

'You want to do it again?'

Whoa. He was asking? What was he thinking, when his face still had that appalled look? 'N…no.'

'Best not,' he said gravely. 'We wouldn't want to give the gargoyles the wrong impression.'

'Right.' She ought to turn round and head inside, she thought, but she couldn't quite get her feet to do the turning. 'So you're never intending to get married? To have kids of your own?' Was she out of her mind, asking questions like this? But they sort of begged to be asked.

'That's why I agreed to marry Maureen.'

'You don't think that maybe one kid might be fun?' Her mouth seemed to be working independently of her head.

'I have five.'

'You made that decision before being landed with five kids,' she said, sticking to her guns. 'No babies.' She hesitated. 'Why do you hardly ever see Ruby?'

'I see Ruby. Once a month I drop in and say hello, or at least I did until I had the kids to look after on my own.'

'A nice formal visit, whether she wanted it or not.'

'Yes. But she does want…'

'Oh, I bet she wants. But do you?'

'Pardon?'

'Do you love Ruby?'

'I owe Ruby everything.'

'Yet you married and adopted five kids, and you didn't tell her.'

'She'd get involved.'

'So you're saving Ruby from herself as well as saving you?'

'You don't have a clue.'

'No,' she said cautiously. This feeling deep within was growing stronger by the minute. This feeling that somehow she'd fallen for this man twenty years ago and had been waiting ever since. It was dumb, but it was there, and it was making her throw caution to the wind. 'But I'm starting to wonder…do you? Ruby lives for involvement. You know she lost her husband when they'd only been married for three years?'

'I know that.'

'And it nearly killed her. But instead of closing herself off she opened herself to every needy kid.'

'As I've done.'

'You haven't opened yourself to anyone. You're still talking about a housekeeper.'

'I can't cope with the kids alone.'

'You want your housekeeper to cope with them alone.'

'No, I don't.'

'But you're still thinking it'd be nice just to see them on weekends. Yet when Wendy doesn't want you it breaks your heart.'

'Hell, Shanni…'

'You don't know what you want,' she said sagely. 'You bought a great big farmhouse cos you thought Ruby might be able to use it to save a few more kids. And then your foster brothers thought Ruby needed to retire, so you went along with that. But it's against your instincts. You know, your instincts were right in the first place.'

'Hell, I was thinking of temporary fostering. Not the full-time care of five—'

'Grandkids. Ruby would treat these kids as grand-kids and, Pierce, these kids so need a grandmother.'

'I won't do that to her.'

'It's what she wants.'

'Then the rest of my foster brothers are right. She has to be protected from herself.'

'Oh, Pierce.'

'Your feet will be getting cold.'

She looked down at her feet. 'So they will.'

'If you don't want to be kissed, then you'd better go back to bed.'

That took her aback. 'If I stay here will you kiss me?' She sounded almost forlorn, she thought. She sounded as if she wanted to be kissed—which she did, with every fibre of her being—but she knew it wasn't going to happen.

For the feeling was gone. What she'd said had been some sort of challenge, and it had made him draw back.

'I need to work,' he said, not answering her question, and she thought it had been dumb to ask. Or maybe it hadn't. Maybe it had forced the end to intimacy.

'Right,' she said.

'Do you still wish to stay here for the two weeks?' he asked, suddenly unsure.

'It's a free holiday.'

'You know we'd be okay if you really wanted to stay with Ruby.'

'Thanks, but I'm staying.' Maybe it wasn't wise, but she was involved, she thought, whether she liked it or not. If she went to Ruby's, she'd spend her time wondering what the kids were doing. What Pierce was doing.

Three days ago she'd been up to her ears in financial and emotional disaster, and now here she was distracted by five needy kids and one needy male.

He wasn't needy. He was a gorgeous hunk, in charge of his world.

He was…Pierce. The Pierce of her childhood. The Pierce of now.

He didn't want to kiss her again.

'I can lend you money,' Pierce said.

There was a moment's stillness.

'You want me to go?'

'I never said…'

'No, but do you want me to go?'

'Hell, Shanni, I just don't want you to get the wrong idea.'

'Because you kissed me, you mean?' Anger came to her aid then, pure, unadulterated fury. 'I'm not a baby. If you think that kiss was something special…'

They both knew it was. But she wasn't admitting it; she'd rather die. 'You're not talking even a one-night stand,' she said, forcing her voice to sound scornful. 'One kiss.'

'That's right.' He still sounded uncertain. 'It was just the one kiss.'

'Actually two,' she reminded him. 'But it's the same thing. One swallow does not a summer make.'

'How the hell do swallows come into this?'

'Beats me.' She backed towards the casement door, clutching her blanket. 'But it seemed appropriate. I'm going to bed.'

He didn't move. 'Goodnight.'

'Goodnight,' she said. She stared at his shadowy figure for a long last moment, but he didn't move.

'Goodnight,' she said again, and turned and fled to her turret bedroom.

One *swallow* does not a summer make? Not even any *swallows*, she thought—plural.

Kisses—plural.

But he didn't have to kiss her. He didn't have to do anything. For, like it or not, stupid or not, she was head over heels in love with Pierce MacLachlan.

CHAPTER NINE

IT WAS a long time before Pierce sought the sanctuary of his bedroom. He'd given up on sleep a long time ago, practically at the time Maureen had arrived needing his help. He'd learned to survive on snatches gleaned where he could. Now he stood motionless, staring out over the sea. Trying to find answers.

Shanni was stirring something inside him that he'd vowed would never be stirred.

Happy families...

His childhood had been one long attempt at happy families. It had been his mother's dream. He'd settle in a foster home, she'd find a new lover, she'd drag him out of his foster placement, and she'd start the happy family routine.

Only of course it was always a disaster. It would fall apart, in weeks or months, but never longer. Then he'd be abandoned again. The foster placement he'd previously been in would almost certainly not still be available, so he'd start all over again. Living with strangers. Trying to make a life.

Once he'd gone to Ruby she'd moved heaven and earth to get him back every time his mother had discarded him, but sometimes even Ruby couldn't help.

Happy families didn't happen.

But now…

He had five children. He'd adopted them. Five children…

And now there was Shanni. A chameleon of a failed art curator, who couldn't paint cows' legs, who made his kids smile, who was orphaned herself…

Let's not get carried away here, he told himself hastily. Her parents were still alive. They'd just sublet their house.

Yet when Shanni had referred to herself as an orphan… It had made him smile, but at the same time it had touched something deep inside that had never been touched. Until now.

He wasn't interested.

She's on the rebound from weirdo Mike, he told himself. That's why she kissed you.

So, why did you kiss her?

There were no answers.

And Wendy had talked to her. For some reason, that hurt. He'd done his best to get close to these kids—well, to get as close as he'd ever want to be—but here was Shanni, diving in as she'd done when she was ten years old, boots and all, tossing her heart into the ring before her…

It scared him to death.

That kiss…

He shouldn't have kissed her. It had changed something inside him, something so fundamental he'd thought it was part of him. To let himself go…

To lose control…

No. Happy families were for others. Not for him. Maureen's plight had wrenched him out of his isolation, but to let him be drawn further…

There was a part of him that was clenched tight with fear. He was falling in love with five kids, and that terrified him. To extend it still further… Hell, he couldn't take that step.

But Shanni…

Shanni. He wanted her so much it was like a physical pain. But to take that step and then lose it…

Maybe he wouldn't lose it. Maybe he could take the chance?

But he didn't trust it. This feeling. He didn't trust himself. Over thirty years of drilled-in knowledge couldn't be overcome by one kiss.

By one slip of a girl.

He shook his head, doubts crowding in from all directions. She was on the rebound. Maybe she always kissed like that. She'd felt sorry for him twenty years ago. Hell, he didn't want pity now.

The doubts were screaming at him. It was like he had six faces before him, the kids and Shanni, all crowding into a heart that had learned early to shrivel in self-defence.

He couldn't. To take that last step…to admit them in and need them…

He'd hurt them. He couldn't give them what they needed. He'd try the best he could with the kids, for he had no choice and neither did they, but to take it further was just plain dumb. Criminally cruel. For he knew Shanni. Twenty years ago she'd been just as she was today—loving, bolshy, demanding. If he let her in, she'd demand more than he could ever be prepared to give.

His love.

He paced the battlements a bit longer, telling himself to move on, but the battlements only went so far. Finally, defeated, he retreated to his vast bedchamber.

Bessy was still asleep. Maybe it was the sea air, or maybe her tiny body had shaken off the worst of the infection and she was sleeping to heal.

He ought to sleep to heal himself.

There's nothing wrong with me, he told the sleeping Bessy, but she wasn't interested.

He was going nuts.

Two weeks…

He had to get rid of Shanni, he decided. She was messing with his equilibrium, and if there was one thing he valued above all else it was his equilibrium. He'd taken on five kids and he'd been crazy to do that. It was done, it couldn't be undone, and he'd do his best for them, but this commitment business went no further. It terrified him.

It couldn't extend to Shanni.

But… She needed a rest. She was broke. She wanted to stay.

He'd asked Blake to help. At the thought of what he'd ask his foster brother to do, he settled a little. It was three in the morning. That meant it was six in the evening in London, and Blake was in London. The international law firm Blake worked with meant he had a base in every major financial district in the world.

Six… Yeah, he'd be still working, Pierce thought. Like the rest of Ruby's boys, Blake was a workaholic. Ruby had launched them with professional qualifications, and past hunger had fed their ambition.

Blake answered on the first ring. 'Hey, Pierce.' From the other side of the world, Pierce's foster brother reacted with pleasure. It was the same for all of them, Pierce thought. Like men who'd gone to battle together, their past meant that they were unfailingly there for each other in a world where they'd learned to trust no one else. 'How goes the menagerie?'

He'd told Blake what he was doing. He'd needed his legal expertise. Blake had reacted with shock, and he had been right behind Pierce's decision not to tell Ruby any more than she'd overheard.

'Great,' Pierce told him now, without conviction.

'Are you at the farm?'

'We're at Loganaich Castle.'

'What, all of you?'

'Yeah.'

There was a moment's pause. Then, 'Hell, Pierce, Ruby will find out about the kids.'

'The staff here have sworn confidentiality. Besides, these people don't see Ruby. She was only here at the opening in her past foster parent role.'

'If you're sure…'

'I'm sure.'

'Cos, bro, much as I love you, if you're in trouble with those kids you're not landing them on Ruby.'

'I won't do that.'

Blake heard the finality of Pierce's tone and backed off. 'I'm sorry. I know you won't. So to what do I owe the pleasure of this call?'

'Shanni.'

'Shanni, as in Ruby's niece? Your temporary housekeeper?'

'That's the one. You got the consent forms I sent you?'

'I did.'

'So I was wondering where it's at.'

'Are we in a rush?' Blake asked cautiously.

'Yes.'

'Why?'

'She's broke,' Pierce said. 'And I'm stuck with her until she's not broke any more. I want her gone.'

There was a moment's pause. 'Um… I thought you needed her for the kids.'

'I don't.'

'Why not?'

'Because the staff here are competent to do any caring that's required, and I don't want her getting any closer to the kids.'

'Because?'

'Hell, Blake…'

'I'm supposed to guess?'

'No.'

'She's pretty, right?'

'No!' Was she? He thought back to Shanni and her pig pyjamas and her blanket. 'A bit.'

'She's gorgeous, maybe?'

'What's that got to do with it?'

'Nothing. I just wondered… So, she's at the castle with you?'

'Yes.'

'And you want to get rid of her?'

'Yes.'

'And you can't get rid of her unless she has money.'

'She's been running this art show in London.'

'I know that.'

'So you've been working on it?'

'I have.'

'And?'

'Too soon to tell, boyo,' Blake said lazily. 'You might be stuck with her for a few days yet.'

'But a promise might be enough to get her off my back.'

'She's really riding you.'

'No. I…'

'You're in trouble,' Blake said slowly, on a note of discovery. 'You've fallen for Ruby's niece.'

'I can't stand her.'

'Why can't you stand her?'

'She's sticking her nose into things that aren't her business.'

'Meaning she's invading your personal space.'

'That too. I tell you, Blake, I want her gone. I need to find a competent middle-aged woman who can give these kids the care they deserve.'

'And Shanni can't.'

'She's a flibbertigibbet. She'll have them fall for her, and she'll be off with the next man.'

'She's a flirt?'

'And the rest. God help us, Blake, she landed in Australia worse than broke. She turned up to work for me without checking the situation. And now she's taking Wendy shopping…'

'I'm missing a few bits here.'

'There's nothing to miss. She's an irresponsible nuisance, and I need your help to get rid of her.'

'I'll see what I can do. And meanwhile…' He paused.

'Meanwhile what?'

'Meanwhile you just take care, little brother. Something tells me you're in way out of your depth.'

'I'm not.'

'Yeah, and pigs might fly. I need to get back to work. See ya.'

The problem with fireplaces was they had chimneys. The problem with rooms back to back in a turret meant that they shared a wall. With a fireplace. With one chimney.

In such a situation sound travelled up chimneys, but on the way it managed a detour into the room behind.

Shanni's room.

'She's an irresponsible nuisance, and I need your help to get rid of her.'

The words made her feel physically ill.

An irresponsible nuisance…

I am not, she told the dark. I cleaned your house and I fed your kids, and I managed to get Donald away from the bull. Where does 'irresponsible nuisance' come into that?

It had been a bit irresponsible to land on his doorstep without checking.

So he'd lied by inferring there was only one child. *That's me being irresponsible?*

Anger helped override hurt. A bit. She indulged

herself in anger a bit more, and found she was so wild she wanted to storm next door and hit him.

Which would indeed be irresponsible.

She should just go. She wasn't wanted. He hated her being here. He'd kissed her against his better judgement, and now he was talking to some stranger, telling him she was interfering in his life.

Right. She'd go. She'd put aside her pride and ring her parents for help. Jules would put her up until her parents could transfer some money.

She was almost twenty-nine years old, planning on sleeping on her best friend's floor until her parents could rescue her. She felt about six.

Anger faded and desolation took over.

She sniffed.

She was an irresponsible nuisance.

So much for imagining she was in love.

So much for being in love.

Her anger had helped but it had faded now. She was left feeling...dumb. And lost. Bereft.

An irresponsible nuisance.

Pierce thought that of her. And she'd been stupid enough to fall...

You don't fall in love in three days, she told herself, but what else was causing this awful, empty sensation in the pit of her stomach?

She wanted to cry. She wanted to sob into her pillow, but maybe Pierce would hear her just as she'd heard him. Knowing his sense of…what? Noblesse oblige? She'd read that somewhere, and it just seemed to fit Pierce. Honourable—except when he was talking to his friend and he didn't think she'd hear.

He'd probably come rushing in to comfort her, and he'd…

Don't go there. Like barging in and confronting him in fury, it might lead… It might lead…

She sniffed again, but very quietly. A girl had some pride even if she was madly in love with a guy who thought she was an irresponsible twerp.

She'd go.

She'd promised to take Wendy shopping.

Okay, I'll do that, she told herself. And then I'll go.

Meanwhile she had to sleep.

She shut her eyes.

The fireplace was just next to her.

Bessy stirred and whimpered, and Pierce whispered into the dark. There were a few more whimpers, a sigh and then the sounds of movement next door.

'Don't cry, baby.' He might just as well have been speaking to Shanni, so immediate was his voice. 'Hush.'

'Hush,' she whispered, echoing into the dark.

'You'll be okay,' Pierce murmured. 'You have two great sisters and two great brothers. That's enough family.'

No, it's not, she felt like yelling, but she didn't. He didn't want her input.

He'd kissed her.

Actually, she'd kissed him.

No matter. He'd kissed her back, and he had no business kissing her like that when he didn't feel like she did. Irresponsibly attracted. Irresistibly attracted.

She groaned, rolled over and buried her head under her pillow.

'Shanni?'

His voice had her sitting bolt-upright.

'Yes?'

'Are you okay?'

'Why wouldn't I be okay?'

'You groaned.'

'I groaned in my sleep. If you're going to listen in on every groan…'

'You groan in your sleep?'

'I must do. I don't know. I was asleep.'

'You sound wide awake now.'

'I was asleep.'

'The sound travels really well through these fire-places.'

'It must do,' she said acidly. 'If you heard me groaning.'

There was a moment's pause, then a cautious, 'You really were asleep?'

'You want a statutory declaration in front of witnesses?'

'When I phoned… Did you hear…?'

'I'm going back to sleep.'

'But…'

'Goodnight.'

'Shanni…'

'Now.'

She lay flat on her back and tugged her pillow back over her face.

Sleep. *Right.*

What had he said on the phone? He couldn't remember. Had she heard?

She'd said she was asleep.

He didn't believe her.

'Da…' Bessy said, and Pierce stared down at the infant in confusion.

'The name's Pierce,' he said.

'Da,' said Bessy.

'Pierce,' said Pierce.

'Some of us are trying to sleep,' Shanni said.

'Da…'

'Fine,' Pierce said bitterly, giving up. 'Call me what you want. Bessy, you talk to Shanni. Shanni, you talk to Bessy.'

'She's your daughter,' Shanni called.

'Da,' said Bessy, and grinned.

Help.

Things were closing around him, things he didn't have a name for. He felt trapped.

Sleep.

Bessy was holding her arms out, pleading to be picked up. The empty fireplace loomed, almost ominously. Shanni was just through there, listening to every sound he made.

'Okay, Bess,' he said wearily. 'Have it your own way. I'll change your nappy and we'll both get some sleep, even if it's in the same bed.'

'Do paediatricians advise babies should sleep in the same beds as their parents?' Shanni asked.

'If you're the expert, Bessy can sleep with you.'

'Oh, I'm not an expert,' she said blithely. 'I'm an independent spirit. I walk alone. Just like you did before you adopted five kids.'

'Shanni…'

'And I'm out of here, just as soon as I've taken Wendy shopping,' she continued. 'You won't see me for dust. So you never have to worry about me kissing you again. *Irresponsible nuisance…* Huh!'

CHAPTER TEN

PLANS for the kids within the castle walls seemed flexible to say the least.

'We have no fixed schedule,' Susie said as they sat around the vast kitchen table the next morning. She was making pancakes. The earl was making toast. Taffy, the dachshund-cum-cocker spaniel, was cruising back and forth under the table waiting for crumbs. 'Every kid who comes here is different and carers have different needs as well.' She glanced at Pierce and then at Shanni. 'You guys both look like you need a good sleep.'

'We don't,' they said in unison, and Susie grinned.

'There's really no need to man the battlements at night,' she said. 'The barbarians were seen off long since.'

'The only thing we need to guard against is pumpkin snatchers,' Hamish said smiling at his wife. 'How big is ours now?'

'Three feet seven inches in diameter on the old scale,' Susie said, with pride. 'We grow competition pumpkins,' she added for the benefit of the confused assemblage. 'You want to see my pumpkin patch after breakfast?'

'I want to go back to the beach,' said Abby. They'd already had a pre-breakfast paddle.

'And so you will,' Susie declared. 'Straight after pancakes.'

'Shanni and I are going shopping,' Wendy said, almost whispering, and Shanni hauled herself out of her own misery to pay attention to the kid over the table. Wendy had ceased to believe in promises, Shanni thought. This kid who'd guarded her family for so long.

She turned and caught Pierce watching Wendy. He was feeling exactly the way she was feeling.

Don't look. Do not think you know what this man is feeling. He doesn't want anything to do with you.

She gulped, turned her attention to the just-arrived pancakes and didn't look up again. But he was watching her now. She knew he was watching her. She could feel it.

She was going nuts.

'Yep, we're going shopping,' she muttered, mouth full. 'Anyone else want to come?'

'I have the plastic,' Pierce said.

She swallowed her pancake. There was a lump that wasn't pancake that refused to be swallowed.

She didn't want to be dependent on Pierce's money. Not this morning. Not ever.

'Hey, shopping's a girl thing,' Susie said, breaking a silence that was suddenly uncomfortable. 'Pierce, accept that you'll be in the way. Shanni, we have accounts with every business in Dolphin Bay. Put it on our tab and Pierce can fix us up later.'

'That's fine,' Pierce said.

He doesn't want to come with us, Shanni thought. Great.

'What's the limit?' she asked him, biting her lip. If she'd been financially independent again she'd say hang the expense.

'Hang the expense,' Pierce said. 'Spend what you need to make my daughter happy.'

It was such a huge statement that they all blinked. Wendy most of all.

'Your daughter...' she whispered.

'That means you, honey,' he said, and rose and ruffled her ragged curls. 'Okay, you and Shanni go and do your girl thing. The rest of us will go to the beach. Okay?'

'Yay!' the boys yelled.

'I'm a girl,' Abby said anxiously.

'So you are,' Pierce said. 'My second daughter. So the choice is yours. Do you want to go to the hairdresser and shop for clothes with Wendy and Shanni, or do you want to help us build sand castles and learn how to ride a boogie board?'

'A boogie board?'

'It's what surfers learn on,' Bryce breathed. 'Cool.'

'Can Taffy come to the beach?' Abby asked.

'Of course,' said Susie.

'Then I'm going to the beach,' said Abby.

'Me, too,' said Bryce.

'Me, too,' said Donald.

'Then that's settled,' Susie said in satisfaction. 'We'll all go to the beach except Wendy and Shanni. Pierce, you drive them into town and then collect them when they're finished. We'll take care of Bessy.'

'Great,' said Pierce, and looked warily at Shanni.

'I can drive my own car,' Shanni said.

'If yours is the Toyota then, no, you can't,' Hamish said.

'Why not?'

'You left the window open last night,' he said apologetically. 'Did you and Donald stop for fish and chips on the way here?'

'We might have,' she said cautiously.

'And left the remains on the back seat?' He grinned. 'Every gull from here to Sydney has been exploring your car. There's enough bird dung on the backseat to fertilize a whole pumpkin patch.'

'Just lucky we have the pumpkin patch to accommodate it,' Susie said cheerfully. 'Don't fret,' she told Shanni. 'We'll have it clean in no time. But meanwhile you need Pierce to drive you.'

'Can't we walk?'

'Not if you want to be back by dinner time.'

'I can drive Pierce's car.'

'I'll drive you,' Pierce growled, and Susie grinned and looked from Shanni to Pierce and back again—and grinned some more.

'I thought you two were friends.'

'He's my employer,' she said tightly.

'Is he, now?' Susie said cordially. 'And here I was thinking…' She broke off. 'But, hey, it's not my job to think. My job's pancakes. But Pierce will be driving you and coming straight back, cos otherwise I'll have to wait at least three hours for my dill pickles and some needs can't be ignored. I'm sure my baby is growing stunted as we speak, owing to a severe deficiency in the dill pickle department.'

They drove into town in silence. Wendy seemed overawed. Pierce seemed almost grim. Shanni was just plain confused.

'You're happy we're doing this?' she demanded as he pulled up in the Dolphin Bay main street. A dozen little shops fronted the harbour. The shops seemed quiet at this hour of the morning—all the action looked as if it was down at the boats.

'I want you to do this,' he said.

'But… You don't want to shop for her yourself?' As if in reply, Wendy's hand came out and gripped Shanni's. Pierce glanced down. He didn't say anything but Shanni knew he'd seen the gesture and it had hurt.

'Girl's stuff,' Wendy whispered.

'But Pierce is paying,' Shanni said to Wendy. 'If he really wants to, maybe he could watch.'

The grip on Shanni's hand tightened still further.

'I won't watch,' Pierce said. Flatly. 'Okay, I'm off to find dill pickles. You want me to pick you up in three hours?'

'At lunch time,' Wendy whispered. And there was an unspoken invitation in her words.

'I'll meet you for lunch, then, shall I?' Pierce asked.

'Great. Here at twelve.' But Shanni felt odd. There was seemingly nothing she could say without tension. She didn't understand it. 'Bye,' she said, because she couldn't think of anything more erudite.

'Bye,' said Wendy and tugged her forward towards the hairdresser.

They walked towards the shops. But Shanni was aware that Pierce was watching them until they disappeared from sight.

They had a brilliant morning. Pure fun. First the Dolphin Bay hairdresser gave Wendy a fantastic elfin haircut and then, inspired, suggested streaks. An hour later Wendy emerged, her copper red hair beautifully streaked with lighter blonde highlights. It might have been over the top for an eleven-year-old, but Wendy had watched in the mirror as her new hairstyle was blow-dryed and her expression made it supremely worthwhile.

'I'm pretty,' Wendy whispered, and the hairdresser beamed.

'I've had to cancel two clients this morning,' she confided to Shanni. 'But the minute I see one of the castle kids come through this door, I drop everything. The whole town understands and nothing's ever given me such pleasure.'

Then they hit the shops, and here the attitude was the same. Wendy was a castle kid, therefore she'd be treated as a princess. Clothes were magically discounted. Extras were added. The lady in the dress shop sent her daughter running to the haberdashery to find matching ribbons for Wendy's new haircut. The youth in the shoe shop was serving someone else when they came in. He barely spared them a glance, but the customer he was serving, an old fisherman, lumbered to his feet, gave the kid a clout across his ears and beamed across at them.

'No, you take the seat, young lady,' he told Wendy. 'You kids come first in this town—Jason here just hasn't realized it.'

They were helped every step of the way, and when she and the beautiful new Wendy—a Wendy dressed in a tiny, bouncy skirt and crop top, gorgeous bright red sandals, and with curls that gleamed—purchased double flavoured ice-creams and sat on the wharf waiting for Pierce, Shanni thought every person in town was finding a reason to peek.

She felt proud. This was a fantastic community, she thought. Surely the community round Two Creek Farm could be the same?

And then Pierce was pulling up nearby and she found she was holding her breath. Wendy had stilled. Her ice cream was held out so she wasn't dripping on her new clothes, but she was no longer licking.

What Pierce thought mattered to Wendy, Shanni thought, and she watched Pierce stride towards them and decided, yep, it mattered to her, too. Once the shadows were dispelled, Wendy would love this man.

Shanni could, too.

Wrong. Shanni already did.

Dumb. She was an irresponsible pest. She had no part in this embryonic family. What she was feeling was a romantic yearning started at ten and never squashed. It had to be squashed now.

Meanwhile, she watched Pierce come towards them and she found she wasn't breathing.

Pierce stopped dead. Thirty feet away, he put his hand to his eyes as if shading them from the sun. As if unsure what he was seeing.

'It's Shanni,' he said, sounding awed. 'But…is that Wendy?'

Wendy giggled. It was a tiny, really nervous giggle, but it was a giggle for all that.

'You're beautiful,' Pierce said and it was exactly right. Not an overblown exclamation. Just a simple stating of facts.

Wendy smiled. She did a coy eyelash flutter. Her smile turned to a beam.

'I'm so proud of you,' Pierce said, and he walked the final few steps and looked down at her. He didn't even glance at Shanni. Which was great. There was no conspiratorial look saying 'haven't we done the right thing!'. It was purely between Wendy and Pierce.

'Can I hold your ice-cream?' Shanni said, guessing what was coming, and then as Wendy didn't answer she took it anyway.

And she was right. Pierce was lifting Wendy high and swinging her round in his arms, so fast that Wendy squealed, a delighted kid's squeal, and everyone watching beamed and beamed.

Shanni blinked.

This was nothing to do with her, she thought frantically. She was out of here.

'Lunch,' Pierce said, setting Wendy down but tucking her against him. 'Unless you're full of ice-cream.'

'My ice-cream's melted,' Wendy said.

Shanni looked down at her hand. She'd forgotten the ice-cream. Yes, it had melted. A blue-heaven-and-raspberry ice-cream was oozing down her hand.

'Oh, yum.'

'Somewhere special for lunch,' Pierce said.

'Fish and chips on the beach?'

'Not today,' Pierce told them. 'There's a great little restaurant up near the lighthouse. We took Ruby there the day of the castle opening. They have champagne.'

'Champagne,' Wendy said cautiously.

'We need to toast a new start,' Pierce said, smiling lazily at her. 'Starting today. But first we need to find Shanni a tap. She appears to be more than a little bit sticky.'

So they found a tap, and then they walked along the cliff path to the lighthouse, Wendy in the middle, one hand holding Shanni's, the other holding Pierce's. It felt…weird.

Pierce had booked. It was a Saturday so the small café was filled with tourists but they were shown to the best table in the house. It had a view seemingly all the way to America. Bench seats were piled high with overstuffed cushions, and bright-striped curtains and wind chimes were everywhere. The place looked like some sort of Middle Eastern harem. Wendy's jaw was down round her ankles, and when the waiter poured champagne into gorgeous crystal flutes she was almost pop-eyed.

'You're too young for champagne,' Pierce told her. 'And you probably won't like it anyway. But it's an important drink for an important toast.' He stood up, raising his glass. 'Here's to a job well done,' he told Wendy. 'You've kept your brothers and sisters safe.

You've taken care of your mum. You've fought off your shadows. This toast is to safety. It's to say you can relax now; you can go back to being a kid. Because I'm doing the caring and I won't let you down. I promise.'

'I'll drink to that,' Shanni said, and stood up and beamed down at Wendy. She felt surreal, like things were moving without her. 'Our brave Wendy.'

'Our beautiful Wendy,' Pierce said, and clinked his glass. Then, as Wendy bravely clinked and sipped and wrinkled her nose, he grinned. 'Before we let you at the lemonade, here's another toast, our Wendy,' he said. 'Here's to Shanni as well, for she braved the bull and more. She braved the ladies of the Craggyburn supermarket. Well done, Shanni.'

It sounded like a conclusion. Now I can bow out, Shanni thought.

But she smiled and clinked her glass. The waiters came and replaced Wendy's champagne with red lemonade. 'How can you like champagne better than this?' Wendy demanded incredulously, and Pierce smiled, and so did Shanni, but Shanni was having trouble making her smile work.

The meal was fantastic. They perused the amazing menu and then somewhat shamefacedly admitted to each other that really they wouldn't mind the fish and chips. So out came the restaurant's version of the humble fish and chips. It was a seafood feast, a vast platter of tiny flathead tails in crispy batter, fresh prawns, juicy scallops under a bed of curling twists of lemon, oysters opened in front of their eyes, mountains of crunchy French fries.

They ate until they thought they might burst, and then they sat back contentedly and watched the coming and going of boats from the harbour, and Shanni thought, *this is paradise*.

'I think it's time for a swim,' Pierce said at last as stillness descended on them and drowsiness took over. 'That is, if we're not so heavy we sink to the bottom with no trace.'

Now. She had to do it now.

'I'm leaving this afternoon,' Shanni said.

There was a stunned silence.

'Leaving,' Pierce said cautiously.

'You can't leave,' Wendy said. 'Where…where are you going?'

'I'm going to visit my friend in Sydney.'

'Who?' Pierce said.

'Jules.'

'I didn't think you had any friends.'

'Hey, I was brought up in this country,' she said with as much dignity as she could manage. 'Just because I've been away for the last few years…'

'You don't have any money.'

'I have enough.'

'What's enough?'

'That's none of your business.' She swallowed. 'Though if you'd like to pay me for the last four days that'd be very welcome.'

'Of course I'll pay, but—'

'You can't go,' Wendy said, horrified. 'We want you to stay.'

'I know,' Shanni said ruefully. She hated doing this; she just hated it. But, sitting between them, she knew she must. For Wendy was already looking at her with trust—and with something deeper. She didn't want to hurt Wendy for the world. To stay here for any longer, to start a relationship she couldn't continue… She couldn't. To leave fast, when the glories of the castle were still before them, was possible. To stay any longer would be selfish.

And there was Pierce. She was falling deeper and deeper in love with them all, she thought desperately, but especially she was falling in love with Pierce, and there was no way Pierce would let that lead to any soppy happy-ever-after ending. She was a nuisance. She had to get out of here.

'You heard that phone call last night,' Pierce said, his eyes not leaving her face.

'Yes,' she said, and jutted her chin.

'Shanni, I didn't mean it.'

'No, but it's true. I'm superfluous.' She took a deep breath. She had to do this. She had to be the strong one. 'Pierce, I want to tell Ruby about these kids.'

'You can't.'

'I can.' In truth she was in territory she didn't understand, but more and more she didn't have a choice. 'I know you don't want to bother her, but believe me the longer you keep this from her the more she'll be hurt. She's already unbelievably hurt that you married and had Bessy without telling her. You're not going to be able to keep things from her any longer.'

She fought for another breath and then turned her attention to Wendy. 'You know, you guys need a proper housekeeper. Not someone like me who doesn't know the first thing about what kids need. Someone who'll love you to bits. Pierce has a lovely old foster mother called Ruby who needs to meet you all. Ruby's like any other grandma—she'd be caring for you in a minute—but I agree, she's too old now to take you on. But if there's one thing Ruby's good at it's networking. She'll find you a housekeeper. She'll be vetted from every angle possible, like you should have vetted me, and you'll be able to get on with your lives.'

'Shanni, you can't.' Pierce sounded horrified.

'I can tell her. Tell your brothers I did it,' she said. 'Sorry, Pierce, but I'm Ruby's niece. Some secrets can't be kept in families and this is one of them.'

'You have no right…'

'Maybe I don't, but I'm doing it anyway.' She rose, feeling shaky. She knew she had to do this because, even though it was tearing her in two now, how much harder would it be if she left it longer?

'Wendy, I'm your friend,' she said, looking down at the stricken little face and flinching. How could she do this? How could she not do this? If she was hurting Wendy now, how much more so if she wasn't honest? 'When you leave the castle I'll come to the farm and see you all. I promise. I'll do the housekeeper thing— I'll fill the house with food and make sure things are okay. I'll see you that day, and I'll see you any time I can find the opportunity. And I'll write to you, Wendy.'

'It's not the same,' Wendy muttered.

'No, but I was your temporary housekeeper,' she said softly. 'My job here is done.'

The journey back to the castle was made in silence. Shanni stared straight ahead. She'd insisted Wendy sit up front with Pierce. She felt small and insignificant in the back seat—and mean.

She'd hurt Wendy. The thought tore her in two. But she looked at the rigid set of Pierce's shoulders and thought, what else was she to do? She had to walk away—if not run.

They pulled into the castle forecourt and sat for a moment, as if each was reluctant to get out.

'They'll be waiting for you on the beach,' Shanni said gently to Wendy. 'Won't they, Pierce?'

'They were planning lunch on the beach when I

left,' Pierce said. 'They've set up a cabana for shade, and they looked set there for the next month.'

'Then you need to get your swimmers on and join them.'

'I want you to come,' Wendy whispered.

'I can't.'

'You mean you won't,' Pierce said.

'That's right,' she whispered. 'I'm mean, selfish…'

'I didn't mean—'

'You know very well why I'm doing this,' she snapped. 'Don't make it any harder.'

He didn't reply. Shanni saw his hands clench on the steering wheel, so hard his knuckles turned white.

'Fine,' he said at last. 'Wendy, let's get our swimmers.'

'But…'

'We have to learn to stick together,' Pierce said harshly. 'Shanni's not part of our family.'

Ouch. But it was true.

'Wendy, I love you lots,' she said. 'I'll come down to the beach and say goodbye.'

She climbed out of the car and fled into the castle before they could say another thing.

In the movies packing was done fast. She'd seen it. The cuckolded husband storming in, seizing his suitcase, throwing in a handful of shirts, slamming the lid and saying, 'I'll be back for the final stuff later.'

Shanni, however, was not a storming kind of

person. She was actually a really messy person. She opened her suitcase and stared at the room and tried to figure out where to start.

She'd only been here twenty-four hours. Hardly time to make herself at home.

Damn, she was crying. She never cried. Never, ever. She sobbed.

Finally she hauled herself together—a little—and marched down to the bathroom to find tissues.

Queen Victoria looked astonished. And even more disapproving.

'Yeah, I'm breaking my heart over five kids and a guy I've known less than a week. Dumb, dumb, dumb.'

No answer. Well, what did she expect? 'You were protected from this sort of thing,' she told the queen. 'Married young, one baby after another…

'You still broke your heart, though,' she whispered, thinking back to history at school, to the stories of the abyss of misery Victoria had fallen into after the death of Albert.

'Yeah, well, you should have found a career you could throw yourself into. Like I have.'

Didn't Queen of England count as a career? And Shanni didn't *have* a career. Thanks to Mike she had nothing, and now thanks to Pierce she had less than nothing—but a cracked heart…

'I thought you couldn't possibly fall in love this fast,' she told Victoria, sniffing hard. 'I was wrong.'

'Shanni?'

She stilled. It was Pierce, calling from below stairs. 'Where are you?' he yelled.

'Talking to Vicky.'

There was a moment's silence, and then the sound of the stairs being taken two or three treads at a time.

The bathroom door was locked. She and Queen Vic were safe.

'Come out,' he called.

'Why aren't you at the beach?'

'I took Wendy down and came back.'

'Did they like her hairdo?'

'They loved it. They're currently making a sandcastle, modelling it on Kirsty. Seeing Kirsty's nine months pregnant it's some sandcastle. Shanni, come out.'

'I'm busy.'

'Talking to Victoria?'

'You think I'm crazy?'

'Hell, no,' he told her. 'Everyone in this damned castle finds a confidante somewhere. Susie told me she's sure Ernst and Eric were marriage counsellors in a former life.'

'Ernst and Eric?'

'The suits of armour at the foot of the stairs.'

She'd forgotten. 'Right.'

'Come out?'

'I don't want to.'

'You sound younger than Abby.'

'Well, then. I'm younger than Abby and a damned nuisance.'

'Shanni, I'm so sorry you heard that conversation last night.'

'So am I,' she snapped, and hauled open the door. Which was a mistake. She'd thought her anger could protect her, at least giving her room to get from the bathroom to the privacy of her bedroom. But as soon as she saw him…

'You've been crying,' he said, and he put his hands on her shoulders.

'I have hayfever,' she said with as much dignity as she could muster. 'I'm allergic to aspidistra. Tell Queen V it's her fault.'

'I don't want you to go.'

'I have to.' She took a deep breath. 'I'm falling in love with…the kids.'

He hesitated. Then, 'Wendy's breaking her heart.'

'I've been with her less than a week. I'm a friend. I'll get over it.' She paused. 'I mean, *she'll* get over it,' she amended.

'So you feel the same?'

'About the kids, maybe, yes,' she snapped. 'They're fantastic. 'You're really lucky.'

'Lucky…'

'Only you don't see that. You're too busy trying to be self-contained.'

'I only know that the kids think you're wonderful.'

'So you want me to stay so you can take even more of a back seat. I don't think so.'

'It's not just the kids.'

She held her breath.

'Look, Shanni, I...'

'Yes?'

'I don't know.' He dug his hands deep in his pockets and swore. 'You cook a mean chocolate cookie.'

'I do, don't I?' She paused, and then softened. Anger was getting her nowhere. He couldn't see what was in front of his eyes—that she was falling hopelessly in love with him, and every minute spent with him was making her more miserable. For he didn't have a clue how to reciprocate such love.

'Pierce, I'm an art curator,' she said gently. 'I'm not a housekeeper. I used you as an emergency stopgap, and now the emergency is over.'

'Is it?'

'Yes, for I've pulled myself together.' She gave another sniff as if to prove it. 'So I'm off back to my world, leaving you to get on with yours.'

'I still don't want you to tell Ruby.'

Great. Back onto neutral ground. Well, it was okay with her—if that was all there was.

'You can't stop me,' she said flatly. 'I won't be a party to hurting my Aunty Ruby. You've hurt her by not telling her about the kids. She knows I've been with you, and I'll be grilled. I won't lie.'

'Just don't go near her.'

'My lovely Aunty Ruby? Avoid her? Like you have for the last year? I love my Aunt Ruby, and you have rocks in your head for suggesting such a thing.'

'She'll give me a really hard time.' He looked so hangdog that suddenly, despite her heartbreak, she chuckled.

'She will, too,' she said. 'I remember when I was twelve I stayed with her. She was having a time out from fostering—there'd been a couple of heartbreaks and she needed time. So my family sent me to keep her company. You remember that white poodle she had?'

'Miffanwy.'

'That's the one. It spent its days preening itself in front of the front-room mirror.'

'So…'

'So I wanted to have a go at dying my hair, but I wasn't game. So I tried it out first on Miffanwy.'

'Oh, God.'

'Flaming scarlet, the packet said, though fire-engine red might be a better description. Anyway Miffanwy darn near had kittens and hid under the bed for days. And I laughed, and Ruby took a mop to me.'

'A mop?'

'She was mopping the kitchen floor when Miffanwy came flying out of the bathroom—bright red—and hid behind her legs. I was giggling and she raised her mop. Well, I went flying out of the house and she chased me and chased me. She was a little tub on legs, without a snowball's chance in a bushfire of catching me. Finally I legged it up a huge eucalyptus in the back yard. Then I was dumb enough to jeer, "You can't catch me."'

'And so…?' he said, and he was smiling. She loved his smile, she thought. She just loved it.

'And so she simply smiled, put her mop back over her shoulder and marched away. "You'll be home for dinner," she said as she left, and I still remember the sinking feeling I had in my stomach as she walked inside.'

'But she wouldn't have hit you.'

'No. Oh, I might have got a faceful of soggy mop and that'd be it. Instead of which, I had to spend three hours every morning for the rest of my holidays scrubbing out kennels at the local dog shelter.'

He grinned. 'Good old Ruby.'

'The punishment fits the crime.'

'It always did.'

'Shanni, stay.'

It slammed back at her. He was still smiling, that wobbly, endearing smile that had her heart turning somersaults. But she wasn't going to be drawn in. She wasn't.

She forced herself to deliberately look behind her. Queen Victoria in widow's weeds looked sternly down upon them. Victoria, who'd fallen so deeply in love that she'd spent almost half of her life in mourning.

And here was Pierce. A man she could fall for, just like that.

A man she had fallen for.

'No,' she said.

'Because?'

'Because you don't understand.'

'Because of the kiss?' he demanded.

'Kisses. If you like.'

He stared at her, baffled. 'Hell, Shanni, no I don't understand.'

'Neither do I,' she said sadly. 'I only know I don't have a choice. I'll go down to the beach and say goodbye, and then I'm leaving. Please, Pierce, don't stop me. I just have to…go.'

CHAPTER ELEVEN

JULES'S floor was really hard. They padded it with cushions, even going out to the shop to buy more, but as a luxury hotel it lacked a certain something.

'It's only until my parents are within phone range,' Shanni reassured her shocked friend. 'They keep going off to digs in the middle of nowhere.'

'Then let me lend you some money.'

'No,' she said, horrified. Pierce had offered her a loan, too. He'd tried to give her far more than her few days' work were worth, but she'd refused to take it. She had enough to feed her for a few more days yet. She'd visited the employment agency— 'We don't get a lot of call for art curators, dear, but if you'd consider waitressing…there's two positions coming up early next week.'

So she lay among Jules's cushions, waiting for the waitressing jobs to happen, or for her parents to come down from their mountains, and she tried really hard not to think of how wonderful a time Pierce and the kids would be having at the castle.

She failed.

'You look like you've been hit by a bus,' Jules said as she flitted in to change on the fourth day Shanni was there. Jules used her apartment as a base for a frantic work and social life. She'd invited Shanni to join her but a round of drinks was higher than Shanni's budget—and how could she drink when she had a broken heart?

'I have a broken heart,' she told Jules.

'Mike was a fink,' Jules said. 'Get over it.'

It wasn't Mike, but she didn't tell Jules that. More questions would ensue—questions she couldn't answer.

On the fifth afternoon at Jules's the doorbell sounded. She was in the middle of watching a particularly gripping episode of *Dallas*. It was rerunning for the thirtieth time, but she hadn't watched it the first time. Or she hadn't watched it much.

She was in her pyjamas.

She nearly didn't answer the door, but then got conscientious. Jules's boyfriend was a romantic who solved arguments with flowers. And they argued often. There were roses in various stages of decomposition all round the apartment. It'd be a delivery person, and surely the least she could do for her friend was accept deliveries.

She stalked over to the door, trying not to think

dark thoughts about best friends with a surfeit of roses. She hauled the door open.

Pierce.

'I thought you were roses,' she said. Stupidly. He looked fabulous, she thought. Hip-hugging, faded jeans. Open-necked shirt with a button missing. His hair doing this floppy thing over one eye. He was a bit sunburned.

He'd been at the beach. Of course he was sunburned. He was…Pierce.

'Roses?' he asked, and she flinched.

'They keep arriving.'

'Roses do?'

'Yes.'

'I'm sorry I'm not roses. Should I fetch some and bring them back?'

'Don't be silly.'

'Okay.' He paused and took in the total package. Bare toes. Pig pyjamas. Hair that hadn't quite been brushed today.

She wasn't absolutely sure that the chocolates she'd been eating weren't evident up there somewhere.

'You have a brown splodge on your nose,' he said. *There you go.* 'What of it?' she muttered.

'You're doing a Miss Haversham for Mike?'

'Miss Haversham?'

'Dickens's bride, who sits in her wedding finery for

ever and for ever, watching mice run through the last vestiges of wedding cake.'

'I'm wearing pyjamas and I'm watching *Dallas*.'

'So you are. Can I come in?'

'It's Jules's apartment.'

'I promise I'll keep it neat.' He looked over her shoulder at the mound of cushions on the floor. Chocolate wrappers. Dying roses.

JR before someone shot him.

'What do you want?' she demanded before things went any further. 'Let's get this on a business footing. Don't count chocolate wrappers.'

He smiled. 'I have good news.'

He shouldn't smile. It messed with her equilibrium. 'The kids are happy?'

'They're missing you.'

'They can hardly miss me when I knew them for less than a week.'

'Yeah.' He looked hesitant. 'I guess. They're having a great time at the castle. The last of Bessy's chicken pox has disappeared. The kids are living on the beach. Oh, and Kirsty had a baby last night. A little boy. They called him Angus.'

'That's lovely.'

'No, Susie says Angus is her name because that's what the old earl was called. But Kirsty says she's loved it for ever, and she met old Angus before Susie did. And Susie's baby might be a girl.'

'So…'

'So all of Dolphin Bay has a view on whether it's right or wrong. The current thinking is that if Susie's baby is a boy they should just call him Earl and be done with it.'

'Right.' She swallowed. Why did she feel he was talking for the sake of talking? 'I… Why aren't you there?'

'I'm surplus. The kids are happy and I needed to come to a meeting in town.'

'So you drove up this morning.'

'And I'm going back tonight.'

'Right.'

Pause. JR was being icily sarcastic from the television behind them.

'You're not depressed, are you?' Pierce asked, cautious.

'No.'

Yet another moment's loaded silence. She should ask him in, she thought.

She couldn't. The idea was just too dangerous.

Scary.

Almost irresistible.

'Would you…?'

'I came to talk to you about Mike.' He cut across her invitation before she could finish, and she blinked.

'Mike.'

'There's news from Blake.'

'Blake.'

'Cut it out with the parrot thing,' he said, and she managed a smile.

'Right. Mike and Blake. What have they got to do with the price of eggs?'

'Nothing, but they have everything to do with your financial situation,' he told her. 'Which is solved.'

'Solved.'

'Hey, didn't I tell you—'

'The parrot thing. Sorry. It's just you're so slow.'

'Blake's got your money back.'

She didn't parrot that. She couldn't. All her breath was knocked out of her.

'You want to know how he did it?' He was leaning against the door jamb looking so sexy she could just melt.

'Of course.' He ought to sew that button back on, she thought. It was doing her head in.

'You had a credit card specifically for paying your artists,' he said, and she somehow hauled her thoughts away from that missing button. Almost.

'Y…yes.'

'So your credit limit was huge. You'd buy and sell on almost straight away. The bank was happy with that because your professional reputation was impeccable.'

She found herself blushing. Ever since she'd met this man she'd felt wrong-footed—a dopy adult-cum-kid who was relying on her parents to bail her out. To have him say that…

'Everywhere Blake enquired he got the same story,' he said gently. 'You're brilliant.'

'But not with money! Or with trusting. She'd given Mike a duplicate and made him a signatory.

'See, here's the thing,' he said. 'Blake used the consent forms you signed to track where the money went. If Mike had blown it at the casino you were up the creek without a paddle, but he didn't. He's astute, your Mike.'

'He's not *my* Mike.'

'No.' Pierce glanced across at JR, who was still not shot. Surely it should be soon? JR was beginning to bug her.

She wanted to focus exclusively on Pierce.

'What he did was buy paintings,' Pierce said. 'Three paintings. Each worth a fortune.'

'So…'

'So we've got them back,' Pierce said, not bothering to hide his exultation.

'You got them back.'

'You're doing the parrot thing again.'

'Will you cut it out?' She was suddenly yelling. The woman behind her was yelling as well. Daytime soap—it had come to this.

She choked on sudden irrepressible laughter, and Pierce looked gobsmacked.

'What?'

'No. Something on telly.'

'On telly.'

'Now you're doing it.'

'Oh.'

'Tell me about the paintings.'

'Blake got an injunction,' he said—with a visible effort. 'On those forms you signed you said the partnership was over the day of the water tossing. Blake cancelled the card retrospectively, claiming Mike had no legal right to use a card in your name once the partnership was void, and anything he did buy certainly shouldn't be his. On that basis Blake got an injunction to seize the paintings, and he moved so fast Mike had no room to object. The paintings will be sold on and used to pay off the card. Seeing Mike bought astutely, Blake seems to think they'll more than pay off the card, with quite a lot left over. Legally you might have to spilt the profit with Mike, but with records showing you were paying him a salary then there's a strong case for the entire profit being yours.'

'Oh, Pierce…' She was suddenly holding onto the door jamb herself. 'Oh…'

'He's good, our Blake.'

'He is.' She wanted to cry.

'Anyway that's all I wanted to tell you,' he said, sounding uncomfortable. 'I'll go.'

She wanted to throw her arms round his neck. *Dammit... Dammit...*

She did throw her arms round his neck. She indulged herself, for one wonderful moment, in burrowing her face in the lovely deep hollow above his collar bone, smelling the clean salt smell of him, feeling his warmth and his strength.

'I don't know how to thank you,' she said, her voice muffled by neck.

But he was putting her away from him, gently but firmly, setting her at arm's length.

'That's fine. You rescued Donald. I rescued you. We're square.'

Right. Why did she feel like sobbing?

'Oh, and the letters you wrote to my foster brothers...'

Whoops. Was this why he was holding her at arm's length? She was so interfering. That was her life skill. To butt into other people's lives, even if in the process it destroyed her own.

'They've accepted it,' he said. 'They don't understand, but they've agreed.'

She'd written to every one of them. Bullied into it, Ruby had given her their email addresses. Blake's, Connor's, Sam's, Darcy's, Dominic's and Nikolai's. She'd said simply that Pierce had adopted five children and had not told Ruby for fear of her wanting to be involved. She'd said that she was

Ruby's niece, that she'd discovered what was going on and that she'd told Ruby. She'd said the biggest way they could hurt Ruby was not to let her share their lives, and that what Pierce had done was cruel. She'd also said their stipulation that Ruby not share her home with whom ever she wanted was leaving Ruby with a lifetime of macramé and no pleasure. So could they please lift their stupid stipulation.

Uh-oh.

'You read it?' she whispered.

'The whole six of them sent it on to me,' Pierce said. 'They've agreed. The stipulation's lifted.'

But there was no pleasure in his words. 'They don't get it?'

'They don't get it.'

'But you do?' She held her breath.

'Maybe I'm beginning to,' he said. 'You've taught me a bit. Ruby and her niece Shanni—taking in the waifs and strays of the world.'

'Hey, it's not me who's taught you anything. I'd have hoped the kids could.'

'How do you mean?'

'If you have to ask then you really don't understand. It's just…' She took a deep breath. 'You know, being part of a family, a proper family, leaves you open for all sorts of hurt.'

'Like when your parents change the locks?'

'Exactly,' she said, struggling to figure out what to

say next. She was feeling more than a little disadvantaged. He was looking so damned sexy and she was in pyjamas. And she was in no position to lecture him when he'd just saved her financially.

'But it'd hurt worse if I didn't *have* them to change the locks,' she said.

'That's because you haven't learned to be independent.'

'I hope I never have to.'

He didn't reply. He was looking at her but he was looking through her, she thought. Holding himself in check. Not making real contact…

'What will you do now?' he asked, and she started, jolted out of preoccupation.

'What do you mean?'

'You've lost the lease on your gallery, but there are others. Blake has contacts in the art world. The story about what happened is already in circulation. I think you'll find it's Mike who's the bad guy in all this.'

'And I'm just the dope.'

'The story doing the rounds is that he swindled you out of what was legally yours. Your artists would be more than happy to start sending work your way again.'

'You have been busy.'

'Blake has.'

'Wow.' She hesitated. 'I'll write and thank him. And try and explain a bit more about Ruby.'

'He still won't understand. And no thanks are necessary. Maybe you could have a drink with him when you go back to London.'

'Maybe I won't be going back to London.'

'No?'

'I don't know. I have this fantastic position here, starting Monday.' No need to tell him it was as a waitress in a railway café.

'Oh.'

'But thanks,' she said awkwardly, and he nodded.

'My pleasure.' He hesitated. 'If you stay…the kids would like to see you again.'

'I have plans to see them.'

'You do?' Was she imagining it or was there eagerness in his tone.

'You know Ruby's interviewing housekeepers?'

'She told me. I knew she'd interfere.'

'She's loving it. Shut up and let her be. So, anyway, the day you come home from the farm… Saturday week?'

'Yes.'

'Ruby's never been to the farm, and she doesn't drive long distances. I said I'd take her down to see it. If she finds someone suitable as housekeeper we thought we'd take her down and introduce you. See if you like her. Maybe we could light the stove before you get home—make it a bit welcoming.'

'There's no need.'

'There is a need,' she said. 'Ruby wants to do it, and for me it'd be a better sort of goodbye.'

'Are there variations of goodbye?'

'Yes,' she snapped, suddenly angry. 'I don't want the last time you see me to be when I'm wearing pig pyjamas and watching *Dallas* with chocolate on my nose. I have some pride.'

'You look cute.'

'I'm a businesswoman,' she snapped. 'A career woman. Not that you've noticed.'

'I've noticed.'

'Then we'll be down there.'

'Shanni…'

'What?'

'I wish—'

'So do I,' she snapped before he could say another word. 'You have no idea how I wish. But it's not going to happen. Now, if you don't mind, I have things to do. I need to wash chocolate off my nose and see whether JR gets it.'

'But…'

'That's all,' she said with a lot more finality than she was feeling. 'Unless you're delivering roses, I'm closing the door.'

And before he could respond she stepped back through the doorway. She looked up at him, half hoping he'd lunge forward and take her into his arms and kiss her senseless.

Or at least say goodbye.

Nothing. He looked blank.

'Goodbye then,' she said herself. She bit her lip. 'I'll see you briefly next week. For a couple of hours. And then that's it.'

It nearly killed him to drive away.

She was so cute she damn near broke his heart. And when she'd hugged him…

Don't go there.

Things were spiralling out of control.

The kids.

That was one area where he was out of control. He'd imagined that he'd take the kids to the castle, hand over their care to the professionals and get some real work done.

He was getting work done, but in ways that surprised him. Sure, Susie and her army of helpers had taken over care of the kids and the kids were gloriously happy. But they'd whoop downstairs on their way to the beach and their cheerful whooping would reach something inside he was trying to block off.

The blocking tactic didn't work. What was happening was that he'd stare down at his plans, double or triple or quadruple his efforts, do what had to be done and then somehow find himself on the beach as well. Sitting in the shallows with Bess on his knee. Holding up small persons as they struggled with this new wonderful skill called swimming. Umpiring beach cricket, or even taking a turn at the bat himself.

They'd come home from the beach tired and happy and sleep as they'd never slept before. He'd hit the plans at night, and his work was sailing.

But all the time he was working…he was thinking about Shanni.

Hell, he couldn't ask her.

Ask her what?

He knew what he wanted to ask her. To be more involved than she already was. To be…

No. Too soon. Far too soon.

And she'd walked away.

Of course she'd walked away, as he should have the minute Maureen had asked him for her help.

And where would the kids have been then?

He swore and concentrated on his driving for a bit. His mobile phone rang. He'd fitted it to the dash so he could take calls when driving. His work colleagues had his number and so did the staff at the castle.

'Yes?'

'Hello, dear.'

'Ruby.'

'I hope it's not an inconvenient time to ring?'

'No.'

'I just want to know the children's sizes.'

'Sizes?'

'For my macramé club. We're having a working bee.'

Agh.

He was being sucked into a black hole, he thought, and there was no control at all. He couldn't even clutch the edges as he slid down.

'Did you see Shanni?' Ruby asked.

'Yes.'

'Did you tell her the good news about her money?'

'Yes.'

'And is she going back to London?'

'I don't think so.'

'That's lovely,' Ruby said, and he could hear her satisfaction down the phone.

'Ruby?'

'Yes, dear?'

'Don't.'

'Don't what?'

'Do what you're doing.'

'Oh, I'm not doing a thing, dear,' she said, and he could hear her beaming. 'You know me. I never interfere. Now just tell me…what are those sizes?'

CHAPTER TWELVE

THE morning they left the castle was heartbreaking. The kids were up at dawn for a last swim. Then they wandered the castle saying their private goodbyes to everything in the place. Pumpkins and suits of armour included.

Pierce said his own goodbye to Queen Vic.

'Okay, large families are fun,' he admitted. 'But they didn't make you smile after you lost your Albert.'

Was it his imagination, or had her expression changed? She looked…somehow more pitying than disapproving.

Weird.

'Look after the aspidistra,' he told her, and made his way down to the breakfast room. Susie's pancake making was well under way. They'd have to learn how to make their own pancakes back at the farm.

Shanni would have made a mean pancake.

Cut it out.

He sat and ate, and the kids chattered, and Taffy begged a piece of pancake from everyone.

'She's going on a diet the minute you guys leave,' Susie said sternly. 'Just lucky she's stretchy and there's lots of her to fill.'

He'd miss Taffy. She nuzzled his hand under the table.

Maybe he could get the kids a dog.

He met Susie's eyes over the plate of pancakes, and she beamed.

'That's a wonderful idea.'

'What's a wonderful idea?' asked Wendy.

'What your father is thinking. Now, there's one more treat…'

'Treat?' The kids' eyes lit up. Every morning there'd been some little thing to look forward to. A sand-castle competition. A trip to the local aquarium. Kite flying. Two days ago they'd all trooped into Dolphin Bay cottage hospital to check out the new Angus. He was jaundiced, so was spending the first few days of his life under lamps. The kids had been enchanted. A new little life…

Pierce had thought of the work Bessy had been, and cringed. But a puppy was a lot less work than a new baby. Maybe.

'You'll cope,' Susie said with understanding, and he blinked. She read him like Shanni did. Dratted women.

'Your today treat is dolphin watching,' Susie said, and he stopped thinking about Shanni. For a moment.

'We didn't think we'd get a treat today,' Donald

said. He was the calculator of the family. The mind. 'It took three hours to drive here. We have to be home by dark.'

'And it's nine o'clock now. You're all packed. Mr Ross who runs Dolphin Bay Charters is picking you all up in half an hour, with your luggage. Mrs Ross will look after Bessy. You guys get to see the dolphins, then Mrs Ross will give you a picnic on the beach, and you get in the car by one. You'll be home by four. All sorted.'

'You won't be coming?' Wendy asked. The kids had learned to love bouncy Susie. They loved her smiley husband and her cute tot of a daughter. They'd miss everything about this place.

'We have to get the place ready for a new lot of kids,' Susie explained, and Wendy's face fell.

'Special kids?'

'Not as special as you,' Susie told her and smiled. 'Kids come in and I look at them and they're just kids. And by the time they go…' Her eyes glimmered for a moment. 'I'll miss you all. You guys come back soon.'

She turned to her pancake batter and stirred with sudden violence. She sniffed.

Here was another one, Pierce thought. Tossing her heart at whoever needed it…

Like Ruby.

Like Shanni.

Didn't they know…?

What?

The thought was suddenly unclear. The argument as to why he couldn't be like that, too.

Bessy tossed a toast crust. It hit him right in the face, leaving a smear of jam over his left eyebrow.

The kids looked shocked—and then they giggled. They wouldn't have giggled two weeks ago. This place was a gift.

Women like Ruby and Susie and…Shanni were a gift.

Enough. He had to move on.

'Okay. Dolphins and then home,' he told the kids, mock-severe. 'And there'll be no more toast tossing.'

Bessy chortled. Pleased with the reaction from the first piece, she tossed again.

Bull's eye!

'Will the balloons stay up until they get here?'

'The instructions say they'll stay up for twenty-four hours.' Ruby was fitting red and gold balloons over the helium cylinder while Shanni tied ribbons. 'I'll sue if they don't last that long.'

'That one's going down already.'

'That's cos you didn't tie it tightly enough. Do you think we have enough sausage rolls?'

'Dwayne's mother's organizing the food.'

'I'm not keen on Dwayne as a boy's name. Do you like my boys' names?'

'I do.' Shanni frowned. 'Did you choose them for their names?'

'Just luck for four of them,' Ruby said. 'But then it got to be sort of a joke. My manly little boys with heroic names. So when I got Connor, Darcy and Dominic as unnamed babies I went straight to my favourite romance novels and found their names there.'

Shanni choked. 'Your babies were named from romance novels?'

'Can you think of a better way?'

'Um…no.'

'And at least they're original. Not like two women fighting over one baby name. Eh, Susie? Eh, Kirsty?'

'Don't bring it up,' Susie said darkly. 'Kirsty, stop gooing over Angus and hand me those streamers.'

There were balloons on the gate.

'There are balloons on our front gate,' Bryce said.

'Look at the balloons,' Abby said.

'Do you think someone's pleased we're home?' Wendy asked. She'd been quiet all the way home. Coming back to the farm wasn't unalloyed pleasure. The kids would have to start school again, and Pierce was aware they'd been given a tough time by the local kids. But what could he do?

'Maybe Ruby's housekeeper is here,' he said cautiously, driving in through a gate that was already open.

'I miss Shanni,' Abby said.

'She was never a housekeeper.'

'She was better than a housekeeper,' Bryce said. Yeah. Pierce agreed with that.

'There's a car parked around the back of the shed,' Donald piped up. 'It's not Shanni's car,' he added.

It looked like…it was! A police car.

What the…?

If he was in for another inquisition…

It didn't fit with the balloons on the gate.

He took a deep breath. 'Okay,' he said, suppressing the urge to turn the car round and head back to the castle. 'We need to find out what's going on.'

'Do you think it might be scary?' Abby asked.

'Not scary,' he said, though when he glanced across at Wendy's set face he wasn't so sure. 'Balloons aren't scary.'

'Housekeepers might be,' Wendy whispered.

'There's only one way to find out,' Pierce said stoutly. 'Let's go and see.

He parked the car. Silence. Not a sound.

They walked forward to the back door. Maybe the balloons had been left as a message of sorts. Maybe.

He went to unlock the back door but it swung open at his touch.

People.

If he'd have to describe that day later on in life, the only word he would find to fit was 'chaos'.

He swung open the door and the place erupted.

There was a cacophony of noise. Bagpipes—someone was playing the bagpipes. Hooters. Whistles. Cheering. Someone was letting off streamer bombs. Someone? Lots of someones.

He backed away but people were tugging him in.

The kids were being picked up and carried into the room.

Susie had Abby. *Susie!*

Hamish had Donald.

Ruby was surging forward to lift Bessy from his arms.

Blake was there. His big brother! Blake was bending down, talking urgently to Bryce, then swinging him up on his shoulders.

Nikolai. Wasn't Nik supposed to be in Mexico?

And Dwayne. The kid from the supermarket. And Dwayne's mum. And the pharmacist. And the doctor. The cops as well. And numerous sun-worn couples he vaguely recognized as neighbours, and their kids, and…

Jake, the Dolphin Bay doctor from the castle was there from the castle as well, with Kirsty and their twins. Kirsty was laughing and holding a blue swathed bundle with pride. And Jodie and Nick. The whole castle team.

Shanni was elbowing her way through the mass, until she reached Wendy.

'Wendy,' she said in satisfaction. She hugged the

little girl, who was clinging to Pierce. 'You're with
me.' Pierce felt her lifted away, but he felt like
hanging on. Wendy might need him.

He might need Wendy.

Dwayne was holding a cake on a tray before him.
Dwayne?

The cake was massive. Vast and chocolate-coated,
surrounded by strawberries, it had great red letter-
ing on the top.

Welcome Home from All of Us.

From all of them.

Pierce stared round the crowded room. There were
so many people that they didn't fit. They were
squeezing themselves in from out in the corridor.
There were people on the back veranda with their
heads in the window.

It sounded like there were people on the roof.

Dwayne's mother gave Dwayne a poke in the small
of the back. He gulped.

'We wanted to welcome your family home,' the
boy managed, talking like he was strangled.
'Um… Mum said…'

'His mum said we've treated you like the pits,' his
mother said stoutly from behind him. 'All of us have.
We had five orphans in our midst and… Well, we
were cruel, and it won't happen again. The freezer's
got so many casseroles in it now that we've had to
borrow Enid Murrihy's second freezer and put it in

the back shed. She says you can keep it,' she added. 'As long as she can put things in when her second daughter's due home. Her daughter's allergic, you understand, so she brings new-fangled food from the city. Enid freezes it and then buries it when Brenda goes home. She's buried tons and tons of wheat-free bread—you wouldn't believe.'

'Mum…'

'Anyway, we just wanted to say welcome,' Dwayne's mother said, getting back on track. 'We've met your Olga and we think she's lovely. Not that Shanni wasn't lovely, but Olga's much more suitable as a housekeeper. She'll always get a discount at our supermarket, and you can't say fairer than that.'

Olga.

To say he was hornswoggled was an understatement. He gazed across the crowd to Shanni. She was dressed as he'd never seen her dressed before—in a gorgeous soft pastel dress with scooped neckline and flowing skirt that reached mid-calf. She looked happy, he thought.

Well, why wouldn't she be happy? She had her money back. She had her life back. She'd go back to London…

Shanni was motioning to a middle-aged lady standing beside Ruby. Olga?

If it was indeed their housekeeper then Olga was different. She was stout and rosy-cheeked. She was dressed in jeans that were a wee bit too tight for her. She was wearing an oversized gingham shirt and boots that came straight out of the Wild West.

'Hi,' she said.

'You're Olga? You're our new housekeeper?'

'I might not be your housekeeper,' she said, smiling nervously as everyone else in the room grinned at Pierce's confusion. 'It's up to you. Ruby knows I've been at a loose end. I used to foster, but then I got done for shoplifting—chocolate, you know?—it was one of the kids' birthdays and my ex-husband had just broken in and taken all the house-keeping money—and I got a conviction and now I'm not allowed to foster, but I'll never shoplift again. I swear.'

There was a moment's stunned silence from the as-semblage. Dwayne's mother drew in her breath on an audible gasp.

'I know you won't,' Ruby said clearly into the silence. 'That's why I said you might be suitable for Pierce.'

'Ruby's the best judge of character I know,' Shanni added.

For some reason all eyes turned back to Dwayne's mother. She took a deep breath. Recovered.

'That's fine, then,' she said gamely. 'If Shanni vouches for you, then it's fine by me. It's still ten-percent discount, and if ever there's a birthday and you're broke then you come to me before you return to a life of crime.'

General laughter. General cheering.

Hey, he hadn't even interviewed the lady yet, Pierce thought, yet the whole community had seemingly accepted her as a done deal.

'Give it up, mate,' Dwayne said softly, still holding the cake. 'It's the women that rule.'

They certainly did. His eyes went again to Shanni. She was watching him. She was laughing, but even so… Her eyes said that she knew what he was feeling.

She'd given him a replacement for her.

'Cut the cake, cut the cake,' people were saying.

'Right.'

'Speech,' someone else said.

'In your dreams.'

More laughter. The cake was set on the table. They cut it as a family, Pierce's broad hand holding the knife, and Bryce, Donald, Wendy and Abby's hands on top.

Someone brought Bessy forward to encourage her to put her hand down, too.

'Da,' Bessy said, and put her fist squarely into the middle of the cake. And then into her mouth.

The party had officially begun.

It wasn't just a party. It was almost a fair, without the profit making. There were donkey rides, apple bobbing, face painting. There were egg-and-spoon and sack races, and toss-the-caber competitions. There was more food than anyone could possibly eat. Pierce moved through the rest of the day as if in a dream, watching the kids—his kids—being embraced by the locals. Being welcomed. Receiving apologies, and promises of largesse from so many people.

For a man who was used to walking alone—who'd spent a lifetime perfecting the art—it was almost overwhelming.

Two of his brothers—Blake and Nik—were here, clapping him on the shoulder, laughing at him, but looking at him with some small concern. His foster brothers had all been raised in the school of hard knocks themselves. Their isolation was an art they valued. Pierce seemed to be tossing it away, and it troubled them.

It troubled him. But…

But he didn't know what.

The kids finally wilted. He took them up to bed and came down again to find clearing up had begun. There was still a party happening outside but inside a team was washing, scrubbing, wiping, gossiping—the farm was alive.

Ruby was in the middle of it, having a ball. She saw him come down the stairs. She laid down her dish cloth and came across to him, and before he knew what she was about she'd enveloped him in a huge hug. Her small, bosomy person held him close, and he felt about six again.

He'd never let himself get too close to Ruby, but she'd always hugged him regardless. Did she know how much those childhood hugs had meant to him?

'Thank you,' he said gruffly as she finally released him.

'It's Shanni you have to thank, not me.'

'You found Olga.'

'She's a treasure. She's as desperate for a family as you were.'

'I'm not.'

'Not any more,' she beamed. 'Oh, Pierce, this is absolute joy.'

'I'm not—'

'Of course you're not,' she said, deliberately cutting across a denial she maybe guessed he was about to make. 'We're cleaning up. You go and find Shanni.'

'Did Shanni organize this?'

'Shanni and Susie. The world's bossiest women. Go find her.'

'Where is she?'

'She said she was going out to talk to a bull.'

'Shanni said…?'

'She said it was a nice bull.'

Hell. He was out of the kitchen before she could say another word, striding through the bunches of people congregated on the veranda, seeking only one person.

He rounded the veranda and stepped down into the garden. Over to the gate to the bull paddock…

She was sitting on the gate post.

Clyde was right beside her.

She wasn't in the actual bull paddock. If Clyde turned nasty she could simply swing herself off the post. Even so, the sight of her beside the great bull made him feel ill.

'Shanni.'

'Hi,' she said without turning round. It was like she was expecting him. 'I've just been explaining to Clyde that I've forgiven him. It wasn't his fault. Dwayne told me what happened. Local kids being stupid. Cruel. Listening to their parents' accounts of wanting you gone and taking matters into their own hands.' She sighed. 'It can happen so fast. To turn you into the local pariah…'

'They never did that.'

'Oh, yes they did. You were lucky they didn't run you out of town with the odd bit of tarring and feathering to go with it.'

'But you changed all that.'

'I just told them the truth. It wasn't so hard. If you'd told them yourself…'

'How could I tell them?'

'Any number of ways,' she snapped, sounding irritated. 'Like for instance stopping to gossip to the ladies in the supermarket. Asking them for the right kind of laundry powder, and admitting you'd been landed with five kids and you didn't know the first thing about laundry. If you'd done that you would have got them behind you, no questions asked, months ago.'

'I couldn't…'

'Open yourself to people? Don't I know it.' She leaned down and scratched Clyde behind the left ear. 'I've just been telling Clyde you're a dodo.'

'A dodo.'

'A very clever dodo.'

'Shanni…'

'Mmm?'

'Will you…?' He hesitated.

She straightened and stared at him. 'Will I what?'

There was another lengthy pause. Shanni had stopped scratching. The big bull tossed his head and nudged her legs. She gave a rueful smile and started scratching again.

'I seem to have given myself a lifetime job,' she whispered. 'Will I what, Pierce?'

He couldn't say. The words that were crowding into his head refused to be uttered.

He'd been sucked into a vortex that was terrifying. No matter what, it seemed he was going down.

His life was no longer self-contained. He had five kids. He had a convicted criminal of a housekeeper called Olga who he just knew was going to end up as dependent on him as the kids were. He had Ruby back on his case. Sometime during the afternoon she'd handed him a parcel—macramé sweaters times five.

And tonight as he'd put Donald to bed the little boy had hugged him. Donald. The last of the kids to accept him.

He'd hugged him back and, damn it he'd felt like crying. He'd let himself in for a lifetime of macramé. And domesticity. The whole catastrophe.

Did he mind?

Maybe not so much, he thought. It was as if he'd been hit by flood water but somehow he'd managed to float. Now he was being swept along, out of control, but somehow he was even managing to enjoy the ride.

But Shanni… She had what he could no longer have. Independence.

'Will I what?' she asked again, and the words that had half formed disappeared from view.

'They're taking orders for coffee,' he said, and he felt her withdraw just a little.

'You came to find me to see if I wanted coffee?'

'Yes. I… And I was worried about you being with Clyde.'

'You think I'd get in the bull paddock? I'm not so dumb.'

'I don't want you taking any risks.'

There was a moment's silence. 'You think I'm a risk taker,' she said at last.

'Yes.'

'I'm not.'

'You throw your heart into the ring.'

'That's risk taking?'

'Yes.'

'But there's good things that can happen because of it,' she said, so softly he had to lean forward to hear. 'I got to toss ice water over naked people, and that has to count as one of life's great pluses. I got my money back, thanks to Blake, the sweetie. You have the most gorgeous foster brothers. Nik has asked me out.'

That was a kick in the gut. Nik. *You bastard...* 'You're not going?'

'I'm busy,' she said with dignity. 'I'm starting a new gallery.'

'In London?'

In Sydney. I'm going to be wildly fashionable, and I'm buying a dog.'

'A dog.'

'Like Taffy. I want one just like Taffy.'

'You deserve something better.'

'Yeah?' She turned to him then, puzzled. 'What could be better than Taffy?'

'I—'

'Having five kids?' She was teasing, smiling down at him in the moonlight. 'And an Olga and a Ruby and a community like this?'

'Shanni…'

'Coffee,' she said and jumped off the post, so suddenly that she caught him unawares. His hands came out instinctively and caught her. Steadied her. Held her close.

She smelled wonderful, he thought. She felt wonderful.

He wanted to…

Shanni…

She didn't move. She stared up at him, seemingly bewildered.

And then she recovered. He saw her face change, as if coming to some sort of conclusion. She gave the tiniest of nods.

She tilted her chin and looked mockingly up at him. She put her hands on either side of his face, and she drew his head down so her mouth could meet his.

For the third time she kissed him.

It wasn't a kiss. It was a dare.

She held him tight against her. She kissed him, like it or not, and who was he to argue? He should, but he couldn't. Any argument was simply kissed out of him.

He didn't move. He didn't respond. Her kiss deepened and deepened some more. Then she was drawing away, just a little, but still holding his face in her hands.

'Coward,' she teased, and kissed him again.

What was a man to say to that? He'd been thrown a challenge. What was a man to do, but kiss back?

One kiss, he promised himself. This night and then it was over. She'd retreat to her life and he'd stay with his.

But meanwhile…

He kissed her as if he'd never let her go. He kissed her as he'd never kissed a woman before, letting go, releasing all his pent-up longing, his aching to be loved, his need to be a part of something that wasn't just him…

She must feel what he was feeling. She must know…

She was the other half of his whole. She was the partner he'd never hoped to find—the woman he hadn't known existed. Shanni…

The kiss went on and on, achingly, heartbreakingly wonderful. He couldn't release her. He mustn't. Shanni…

'Coffee!' The yell was loud enough to wake the dead. It was Dwayne, yelling into the darkness, straining to see beyond the pool of light cast by the lanterns on the veranda.

'Hey, guys, come and get coffee. And Shanni, Ruby says are you going to drive her home, cos if you don't come soon she's sleeping off the champagne here and now. And Mum says everyone can stay for breakfast if they want, but there's not enough eggs.'

And that was that.

They broke apart. Rational thought prevailed. Sort of.

Shanni took a step back and gazed up at him in the moonlight. She looked bruised, he thought. Confused. Frightened?

Yeah, frightened. He couldn't bear it. He put a hand on her cheek lightly, a feather touch.

If he was falling for someone with the encumbrances he had, he'd be terrified as well.

'Hey, don't look like that. I'm not asking anything of you.'

'No?'

'It doesn't mean anything.'

'What doesn't?'

'Kissing.' He had to say it. Dwayne was still staring down into the darkness. Any minute now he'd get sick of staring and jump down and make certain it was them.

'It's just…kissing?' she whispered.

'Of course it is. What else could it be?'

'You don't want…?'

'Hey, I have enough encumbrances,' he said, trying to keep his voice steady. 'I'm not in the market for more.'

The fear he'd seen—or had he imagined it?— faded. It was replaced by bleakness. And maybe a little anger.

'I guess I'm not either,' she managed.

'You're setting up an art gallery in Sydney.'

'So I am.'

'It'd never—' He paused. 'No.'

'It might,' Shanni said urgently. 'Pierce, it might.'

'I don't do relationships.'

'No?'

'No,' he said flatly and then again as if it needed accentuating. 'No.'

'But you're father to five…'

'Yeah, so isn't that enough?' He hesitated, but it had to be said. He might be falling in out of his depth, but he was damned if he was dragging her down with him. 'Get out of here, Shanni,' he said gently. 'While the going's good.'

'You mean cut and run?'

'Yes.'

'As you'd like to do?'

'Yes.'

'Would you really like that? To be free again?'

'Of course.'

There was a moment's silence. 'Coffee?' Dwayne called again from the veranda, sounding unsure. He'd assumed they were out there but he couldn't hear them.

'I don't—' Shanni said, and then she stopped. 'Pierce…'

'No,' he said, so forcefully that Dwayne heard.

'It *is* you,' he said from the veranda. 'Everyone's looking for you. Mum says do you want her to come back at breakfast time and bring eggs?'

'No,' Pierce said again.

'No?' Dwayne sounded confused.

'Everyone's going home,' Pierce said, but his eyes didn't leave Shanni's.

'Everyone?' Dwayne asked.

'Olga can stay,' he said.

'That's magnanimous of you,' Shanni muttered. 'Your brothers have come from overseas.'

'You sent for them.'

'Ruby did. She said she was worried about you, and before we could blink they were in the country.' She hesitated. 'Blake's been magnificent. And...' She took a deep breath. 'Nik is cute.'

'Don't you dare go out with him.'

'Why not?'

'He'll break your heart.'

'Not possible.'

'Of course. Mike's already broken it.'

She flinched. Then, 'You know, I thought for a bit that he might have,' she said. 'But I didn't know the first thing about loving. And I sure as heck didn't know the first thing about broken hearts. It's taken an expert to teach me.'

'Shanni...'

'If you really don't want me, then I'll go,' she said, and she broke away. 'I'm coming, Dwayne,' she called. 'And your mum doesn't need to worry about eggs. There's enough food in the kitchen to feed Pierce's immediate family and he has no intention of expanding it.'

She left soon after. She helped Ruby into the car, and the two of them headed off, with only Ruby looking back.

'I hate to leave,' Ruby whispered as the lights from the farm faded from view. 'It seems wrong.'

It did seem wrong. Shanni's face was set. Ruby glanced at her cautiously and then looked away.

'I'm sorry, dear.'

'It's not your fault he's a pig-headed, independent, bottom-feeding maw worm.'

'You've got it bad,' Ruby whispered.

'I have,' Shanni agreed and didn't say anything.

'You love him very much?' Ruby murmured after a while.

'More than life itself. Almost more than I love his kids.'

'Oh, Shanni…'

'But I'll get over it,' Shanni muttered. 'I have to. And Mum and Dad get home tomorrow. Yay, I'll get my bedroom back. I'm in extraordinary need of Susie Belle.'

'Pierce?'

He was back standing against the post where Shanni had sat. Even Clyde had deserted him.

Behind him, the house was in silence. The partygoers had gone. Blake and Nik were still here, as was Olga, but he'd said goodnight and left them. He'd assumed they were asleep.

But not Blake. Blake was two years older than Pierce, and he'd taken on the role of eldest sibling.

'There's a beer back here on the veranda,' he called.

'I don't need a beer.'

'Yeah, you do,' Blake said easily. 'You've hardly had a drink all night. You've looked like you were being chased by demons. Everyone else has had a ball, and you've looked like you were being chained and tossed into a dungeon.'

'Hell, I didn't…?'

'Oh, you smiled,' Blake said. 'No one who didn't know you well could guess.'

Should he say he hadn't guessed himself until Ruby had grabbed him on the way to the car? 'Talk to your brother. He's in love with Shanni and he won't admit it,' she'd said.

Talking personal stuff didn't come easy to any of them, but for Ruby's sake—and for Pierce's—he guessed he'd try.

So Blake tugged a couple of ring pulls and they drank beer and stared into the night for a while. Pierce had turned off all the outside lights and Blake hadn't turned them on again. There was only the moonlight. And silence.

'Ruby says you're in love with Shanni,' Blake said at last, and Pierce almost choked on his beer.

'What the hell?'

'She says you've got it bad. But you're being stubborn.'

'What does she know?'

'Of all the people in the world, maybe it's Ruby who knows us best,' Blake says. 'She's seen us at our worst. She took us in and loved us, regardless.'

'She's great.'

'Shanni says we have to toss out the stipulations on her apartment. She says it's cruel.'

'Shanni's right.'

'She's quite a girl,' Blake said cautiously. 'Mind, she's Ruby's niece, so she has a head start. Nik is really taken with her.'

'Tell Nik to leave her alone.'

'Tell him yourself, little brother. And, if you don't want her, what's the problem?'

'She deserves better...than us.'

'What's wrong with Nik? He scrubs up quite well. You've seen him in a suit. He earns a fortune. Some women would describe him as a catch.'

'Yeah, but you know us. We don't do...the love bit.'

'I'm seeing you come pretty close,' Blake said cautiously. 'Five kids. What the hell were you thinking?'

'If you'd met Maureen you wouldn't ask. There was no choice.'

'No.' He hesitated. 'I guess there wasn't. But after it was a done deal, you could have packed them all back to Sydney. You'd get housekeepers there. You could have organized a crèche and after-school care. You could have stayed almost as independent as you once were. But you stayed here, boyo. Something inside must have seen what these kids needed.'

'That's Ruby talking.'

'Yeah, it is,' Blake agreed ruefully. 'She said your independence is shot to hell and you're in love with Shanni, and why don't you ask her to marry you and be done with it.'

'Because she'd say yes.'

Hmm.

Blake concentrated on his beer for a moment. Pierce stared out into the darkness, listening to his words echo in his head. He'd said it. The unthinkable.

'You think she might love you back?' Blake asked, and Pierce thought, *he's not asking if I love Shanni. He's assuming it. Was it that obvious?*

'She might,' Pierce said at last. 'She's a soft touch.'

'She's a nice kid.'

'She feels sorry for me.'

'Hey, I saw her watching you when you carried the kids up to bed,' Blake said. 'I'm pretty impervious to sentiment, but what I saw on her face wasn't pity.'

'No?'

'Pure unadulterated lust, mate,' Blake said with satisfaction. 'Should be more of it. You think she's hot? She's besotted. So... You're stuck here with five kids. One wife's not going to make much difference, and it might make both of you happier. Come on, bro. It's happy families. You've got the babies. Now you need the bride.'

'You think I'd lay that on her?' he snapped, revolted.

'Why the hell not?'

'Because she's generous to a fault. She feels desperately sorry for the kids. She knows just how they feel—she has Ruby's sixth sense. She's just like Ruby. She tosses her heart into the ring without thinking of the consequences. She's a brilliant art curator. To ask her to marry me and be saddled with five kids and their associated baggage...'

'She can always refuse.'

'She wouldn't. She couldn't. She's too dammed soft-hearted.'

'So you're going to protect her like we tried to protect Ruby,' Blake said. 'Yeah, like that worked. We made Ruby miserable. It was Shanni who made us see. Surely you could give her the benefit of the doubt—that she's an intelligent woman who knows you're set up with a housekeeper and that you're not asking her to scrub and bake?'

'But she would scrub and bake. I know Shanni.'

'Then surely she should be allowed to?'

'Hell, Blake, if you were me would you ask her to marry you? I'm under a huge debt to her as it is. I won't be obligated to her any more.'

'You think she'd be doing you a favour, marrying you?'

'Of course she would.'

'Ask her and see what her reaction is.'

'No.'

'You want me to ask her?'

'Don't be daft.'

'No, I mean it. I could just have dinner with her and run the idea past her… As sort of a hypothetical… "Would you ever consider marrying a man with five kids and a chip on his shoulder the size of Ayer's Rock?"'

'No.'

'Or Nik could ask.'

'No!'

'Then ask her yourself.'

'No to that, too,' Pierce said bleakly. 'What sort of life would I be asking her to share?'

'A chaotic one, I'd agree,' Blake said, finishing his beer and standing up. 'But surely she has the right of refusal?'

'I'm not asking.'

'Have it your own way,' Blake said, holding out a

hand and hauling him to his feet. 'Ruby asked me to say all this, so my job here is done. But the way I see it you're in love with her. And if you don't ask her to marry you, someone else will.'

'Someone else is welcome to.'

'Nik?'

'I'd kill him.'

'Yeah, well, she'll marry someone,' Blake said. 'If you won't let me intervene, talk to Ruby.'

'No.'

'You don't want to marry her?'

'Of course I do. But I'm not asking. She has a life.'

Silence. The old house seemed to slumber.

But upstairs on the box seat, under the girls' bedroom window, Wendy sat in her nightdress hugging her knees. Her bedroom window was wide open. Right over the place where Blake and Pierce had shared their beer.

'If you don't ask her to marry you, someone else will…'

'I'm not asking.'

She hugged her knees some more. Then she climbed back into bed and tried to close her eyes.

'If you don't ask her to marry you, someone else will…'

'I'm not asking.'

The night stretched out before her.

'If you don't ask her to marry you, someone else will...'

Who?

CHAPTER THIRTEEN

HE WOKE and there was a deputation standing around his bed.

Abby. Donald. Bryce.

He winced. He glanced at the bedside clock and winced again. It was just after six. It was two when he'd finally got to bed, and he'd been up once with Bessy, who'd wanted to be entertained.

Bessy was now sleeping. With luck she'd sleep for a couple more hours.

'It's really early, guys,' he muttered, but without conviction, already knowing his night was over.

'We can't find Wendy,' Abby said.

'And she's made her bed and left a note,' Donald added.

He sat up. Wide awake.

'Here's the note,' Donald said and handed it over. His small face looked terrified. 'It's three hundred and twenty nine kilometres to Sydney.'

What the hell…?

He stared at Donald. And then he stared at the note.

I've gone to see Shanni. I have something really important to ask her—stuff I can't tell Pierce. She gave me her address so I know where I'm going. I'll ask Shanni to phone you when I get there.

'When did she go?' he whispered.

'We don't know,' Abby whispered back. 'I woke up and her bed was made so I went to see the boys.'

'I felt her sheets,' Donald said. 'They're cold.'

Dear God. The bottom seemed to sink out of his stomach. He stared at the surrounding children and saw his reaction mirrored in their eyes.

Wendy. The reliable one.

Walking to Sydney?

He dropped the note and reached for his jeans. 'Blake! Nik!' He erupted from the bedroom, bellowing for his brothers. Behind him, Bessy stirred into instant wakefulness and started to roar.

He couldn't pay her heed. What were brothers for?

'Get the hell up. Blake. Nik. Olga!' By the time he reached the foot of the stairs, he'd hauled his windcheater over his head. He was groping in the pile of shoes habitually left in the porch as his brothers stuck sleepy heads out of the rooms where they'd been sleeping. Olga appeared from down the hall, wreathed in curlers.

'Is it a fire?' Nik demanded. Then a worse thought

struck. 'You're not heading out to milk cows, are you? Cos if you are, there's limits to brotherly love.'

'I'm going to find Wendy,' Pierce said, and he was already heading for the door. 'She's trying to get to Sydney. Hell, it's impossible. Look after the kids. Kids, I'll be back the minute I find her. I promise.'

'Do you have your phone with you?' Blake was awake enough now to lurch forward and grab his brother by the windcheater. 'Where's your mobile phone?'

'He doesn't carry it cos work rings up when Bessy's crying,' Donald said from the top of the stairs. 'It's in the charger. I'll get it.'

'She's out there…'

'Yeah, and if someone finds her and brings her home we need to be able to tell you,' Blake said. 'Nik, go with him.'

Nik was wearing boxer shorts, a stunned expression and nothing else. 'I'm not waiting,' Pierce snapped.

'Okay, tell Nik where to look. Do we know where she was heading?'

'Shanni's.'

'Does Shanni have a phone?'

Did Shanni carry a phone? Hell, how would he know? She'd still be with… Jules. Or Ruby? 'Maybe…'

'I'll ring Ruby and find out,' Blake snapped. Donald hurtled down the stairs and handed him the phone. He tossed it to Pierce, who took off towards the car as if he'd just been handed the Olympic baton.

'Where will you look?' Blake yelled.

'She'll be out on the highway. This is a dead-end lane. If she's out there…'

'Okay, bro, go. Head for the highway towards town. Nik will double check the lane and we'll search here. And answer your phone when it rings.'

'Will do,' Pierce yelled. 'Bessy needs changing.'

He was gone.

The drive from the farm into town was one of the longest journeys of Pierce's life. There was no other way to get to Sydney—Wendy would know that. She'd have to walk into town to reach the highway. It would take her hours to get there.

Had she had hours?

And then what? There were buses, but she didn't know the timetable. She didn't have any money. Or did she? Surely she wouldn't have taken…? He pulled over and rang home.

'Check my wallet,' he demanded.

'Where?'

'Bedside table.'

'It's full,' Blake reported seconds later. 'A hundred and fifty bucks in notes.'

It hadn't been touched. So she was broke. Pierce drove on, feeling desperate. The closer to town he got, the sicker he felt. She couldn't have walked this far. She couldn't have called a cab—there were no cabs out here anyway.

Maybe she was hiding, but this was open country. Huge red gums in undulating paddocks. Clear verges. Nowhere a child could duck to hide from a passing car.

By the town boundary he was feeling just about as bad as it was possible to feel. And then some.

His phone rang.

He stared at it. Almost afraid to answer.

He pulled over and picked it up like it was poisonous.

'She's safe,' Blake said, and the air in Pierce's chest whooshed out like he'd been hit in the small of the back.

'Safe.'

'She's at the police station, boyo,' Blake said. 'A milk tanker driver saw her with her thumb in the air. Hitch-hiking. He's a family man, and he had enough sense to take her straight to the cops. She's waiting for you there. She's safe.'

'Shanni?'

Shanni was sound asleep in Ruby's spare room. She was asleep because she'd paced until five a.m. It took more than half a dozen rings before she realized her mobile phone was ringing.

'Hi,' she said, still half asleep.

'Shanni?' A deep male voice she didn't recognise.
'Yes?'

'It's Constable Bob Lester here, from the Craggyburn Police. You remember you gave me your number a few weeks ago?'

'Yes,' she said, trying to focus. Oh, great. A policeman waking her at dawn to ask her for a date. 'Um...what can I do for you?'

'I have someone here who'd like to talk to you,' the policeman said gently. 'Here you go, Wendy. She's all yours.'

Wendy was sitting in the back of the police station, in a lounge the officers used during breaks. She was drinking hot chocolate, her eyes enormous over her mug.

The constable opened the door and she cringed.

Pierce thought his heart would break, right then and there.

'Wendy,' he whispered, and she put her mug very carefully on the table and lifted her chin. Defiant. Only it didn't quite work. Her chin wobbled and sank again. She was still a very little girl.

'Are you mad at me?' she whispered, and it was enough.

He was over at the table, kicking a chair aside as if it was presumptuous enough to get in his way. He was hugging her, holding her tight against him, burying his face in her lovely short curls. Damn it he was weeping.

'She's okay,' the police constable said from behind him, and he fought a bit for composure, hugged Wendy a bit more and then managed to put Wendy far enough away from him so he could see her face.

It was as tear stained as…well, as his must be.

'I'm sorry,' she whispered.

'There's no need to be sorry. We have you safe.'

'She'd been walking for hours,' the constable said with a hint of reproof. 'No one uses that road at that hour of night. The milk tanker starts at six and he found her on the first run. She had her thumb up like a real hitch-hiker. Then, when he stopped, she ran away.'

'He… I was…' Wendy tried to make her voice work, but failed. She was terrified. Her whole body was shaking. This child had learned the hard way that men weren't to be trusted.

'He didn't know what to do,' the policeman said. 'But he thought, well, he chased her and caught her and brought her here. By the time he brought her in he had her calmed down a little—apparently he has a kid in her class at school—but she was scared witless.'

'Hell, Wendy…'

'I wanted to go to Shanni.'

'I organized that at least,' the cop said. 'Before I rang your place I let her ring Shanni.'

Pierce was having trouble taking it all in. 'You rang Shanni?'

'If she'd gone to all that trouble, and we'd stopped her running away, the least I could do was let her phone.'

'Did Shanni give you her number?' Pierce asked Wendy, and Wendy shook her head and buried her face in Pierce's shoulder again.

'It was me,' the cop said, a bit shamefaced. He motioned to a bit of art paper lying on the desk. 'Shanni gave me her number a couple of weeks back. I was going to use it, too,' he muttered. 'But she was so caught up with all those kids. I'm not a family man.'

Pierce took Wendy home. She said little, huddled into the passenger seat as if still frightened, looking far younger than her years.

He couldn't figure out the why, and she wouldn't say.

'I just had to ask her something,' she whispered and that was all she'd say. 'I'm sorry.'

'Wendy, if you ever want to ask anyone anything— if you ever want to visit anyone—just ask me. I swear I'll take you.'

'I know. But I needed to talk to her by myself.'

Even at home she wouldn't talk. Olga took one look and showed her true colours—born mum.

'The rest of you leave her alone. She's had a nasty shock—anyone can see that. And look at those feet…walking all that way in sandals. Even though they are pretty. Into the bath with you, sweetheart, and Abby you come and sit beside her while I wash her. You.' She turned on Pierce. 'You make her a lovely soft egg with toast soldiers. We'll feed it to her in the bath.'

'Toast soldiers,' Pierce said blankly.

'Hey, even I know that one,' Nik said, grinning. They were all grinning. 'Hell, bro, you have a way to go in the parenting stakes.'

Wendy soaked in her bath. She ate her toast fingers and then Olga popped her to sleep on the ancient divan in the corner of the kitchen.

'For you don't want to be alone upstairs,' she said. 'The rest of you, shoo outside while I do some baking.'

'Abby,' Wendy whispered.

'I'll lie down with her,' Abby volunteered, and Pierce thought his heart would break all over again.

'There's naught for you to do here,' Olga told him, the way her words softened on the order telling him she understood a little of what he must be going through. 'Go round up some cows, or whatever you do with cows.'

'Hey, teach us,' Nik said.

'Aren't you two going back to wherever you come from?' Pierce demanded.

'Hell, no,' Blake said. 'We're waiting for the next instalment.'

Which happened approximately two minutes after they'd cleared the main course of Olga's delicious roast lunch, and just as she was cutting and serving the apple pie.

Wendy was deeply asleep in the corner. Bessy was tossing food indiscriminately round her high chair. Everyone else was at the table

Shanni walked in. She looked like Pierce had that morning—jeans and windcheater—and she hadn't taken time to brush her hair.

Dazed.

'Hi,' she said.

There was an awed silence.

'Shanni,' Pierce said stupidly.

'Shanni,' Abby yelled, as if she hadn't seen her for a year. 'Shanni's here. Wendy, wake up, Shanni's here.'

'Why are you here?' Pierce asked, trying to get his voice to work.

'I'm here to ask if you'll marry me.'

Pierce had been spooning creamed apple into Bessy's mouth. His hand had locked, spoon halfway to Bessy's mouth.

Around the table everyone else stayed frozen. But they all recovered before Pierce did.

'Goody, I want to be flower girl,' Abby said in a

voice of profound satisfaction. 'Donald, you're not allowed to take all the cream.'

'Cool,' said Nik, shifting along the bench seat to make room. 'You want some lunch?'

'I bet you haven't eaten.' Olga rose and moved ponderously to the stove. She was still in her curlers and an amazing oriental housecoat, purple and black shimmering silk with deep pink tassles. 'There's still some roast. Or do you want to move straight to apple pie?'

'Let the boy answer first,' Blake said, and they fell silent again.

'I don't...' He stared at Shanni. 'I don't understand.'

'Wendy said you want to marry me,' Shanni said. She hadn't moved into the room. She was standing in the doorway, looking only at Pierce.

In the corner Wendy was waking. She didn't move, curled into a warm little ball under the feather eiderdown Olga had spread over her. But her eyes were suddenly wary.

'Wendy says the only reason you won't ask me to marry you is that you don't think I want the children,' Shanni said. 'But Wendy says she'd look after the kids. She's offered for them all to go into a care home—but please will we visit.'

There was an almost audible gasp. All eyes moved to Wendy.

'It's...it's true,' Wendy whispered from the sidelines. 'The child welfare officers say there's houses for families as big as ours. We get care workers. And I thought…maybe we could come here at weekends. Sometimes.'

'How about you stay here?' Shanni said, suddenly sounding fierce, and blinking a bit. 'How about if I just move in and we keep on like it is now? Me and Pierce and Olga and Wendy and Donald and Bryce and Abby and Bessy. And anyone else we can think of.'

'You can't,' Pierce managed.

'Why can't I?'

'Your career.'

'Stuff my career,' she retorted. But then she grinned. 'But, in case you hadn't noticed, this is a tourist district. It's very, very trendy to come for a Sunday drive and visit art galleries. There are gallery owners in Paddington or The Rocks in Sydney who are moving to the country because they get more clientele that way.'

'It's not so much of a tourist district,' Nik said, thoughtful.

'It will be,' Shanni said, and tilted her chin. 'When people hear about the fantastic art gallery I'm going to open.'

'Dolphin Bay would be better,' Blake said.

'Sorry?' Distracted from Pierce, Shanni looked to his brothers.

'It'd be better at Dolphin Bay,' Blake said. 'It's screaming for a bit of culture. Money's not a problem. Nor is commuting for Pierce. There's a train, and he mostly works from home anyway. But you'd get many more tourists in Dolphin Bay. You could buy a big home there and open the world's best gallery while Pierce keeps on with his architecture. And you could use this place for holidays.'

'Sorry?'

'Hey, it could be more than that.' Nik was putting in his oar again. 'I was talking to Hamish at the opening of Loganaich Castle. And Ruby. They had this vision of there being a network of places that could be used for disadvantaged kids. Or more, for families in crisis. Single mothers who are having a dreadful time. We could set this farm up to do the same thing. Us guys. The seven of Ruby's boys. We could put in enough to make it work. We could call it Ruby's Farm. She'd love it.'

'What the hell…?' Pierce was having trouble getting a word in edgeways.

'We'll do it.' Nik said enthusiastically. 'We'll get you out of here and then we'll change a few things. We might have to shift Clyde further from the house and put in a few more kid-friendly animals. Ponies. A couple of nice cats and a fat old dog. And get some lovely kid-friendly housekeeper, and a couple of kid-friendly helpers.'

'I could be that,' Olga said breathlessly. But then she looked at Pierce. 'But no. I want to stay with you in Dolphin Bay. I have a friend, Maybeline, and she could come here. She had a farm before her husband took off with another woman and made them both bankrupt. She loves kids.'

'And Ruby wants to move to Dolphin Bay,' Blake added. 'She told me. Apparently there's a really good macramé club there. So all you need to do is find a big house there and you're home and hosed.'

'I think Ruby should have her own home, though,' Nik said. 'A cottage.'

'Near your house, though,' Blake added.

'Excuse me,' Pierce said and stood up.

'Don't you want to marry Shanni?' Abby said in a small voice, and everybody hushed.

Shanni looked at him.

He looked at Shanni.

'Yes,' he said, and the collective breath was let out in a collective sigh.

'But I need to ask her,' he said.

'No need,' Blake said. 'Job's done. Olga, can you pass the pie down here, please?'

Pierce was in the middle of the table. Olga handed him the pie. He handed it on to Blake without thinking.

Shanni was looking confused. The rest of them had moved on, distracted by what looked a truly excellent pie.

It was a great pie.

'Leave some for us or you're dead meat,' Pierce growled.

'If you're going to propose, then hurry up and do it,' Olga urged. 'Blake, that slice is too big. Nine equal portions. You cut and the rest of us choose.'

He took her out to Clyde's paddock. The big bull was on the far side looking longingly at the cows beyond his boundary. Here at last was privacy.

Pierce had Shanni by the hand. He marched Shanni out to the gate and stopped.

'You seem…angry,' Shanni said tentatively, and he turned and faced her.

'Exasperated, more like.'

'Why?'

'I like a bit of control.'

'Me, too,' she said.

'So we have something in common.'

'Something more than love for five kids?'

'You love the kids?'

'Of course I do,' she said. 'What's not to love?'

'Do you know how many times I get to sleep right through the night?'

'Sleeping's boring.'

'Do you know what you're letting yourself in for?'

'It'd be okay,' she whispered. 'If…'

'If what?'

'If you loved me.'

The world stilled.

'What makes you think I don't love you?' he said at last.

'You've never said.'

'I don't know how.'

'How to love?

'No.'

'It's easy,' she said, and it was her turn to sound exasperated. She linked her arms around his neck. She stood on tiptoe. She kissed him, ever so lightly on the lips, and then pulled away a little before he could respond.

'This is how,' she whispered. 'Pierce MacLachlan, I love you. I love you from the tip of my toes to the top of my head. I love you more than I ever thought I could love anyone. I love you even more than I love Susie Belle.'

'Susie Belle?'

'You haven't met her. You will. She's about to make our Wendy very happy.'

'*Our* Wendy.'

'She is our Wendy,' she whispered. 'Our gorgeous little girl. The bravest kid. I love her so much.'

'How much love have you got?' he demanded, and she chuckled.

'It just keeps on oozing out. I blame the ice water. It was sort of a cathartic experience. It released the inner me.'

'Shanni…'

'Yes, my love?' She was still on tiptoes, still within kissing distance, still holding him.

'I don't know about the love thing.'

'You don't think you can love me?'

'It seems I can,' he said, sounding dazed. 'It seems I do.'

'But?'

'I didn't think I could do it. I'm still not sure.'

'Okay, here's a test,' she said, kissing him again. 'I'm moving in here anyway. I love these kids to bits. Ruby's met them for one night and she loves them. So does Olga. You've just reclaimed a whole lot of money for me—so I can rent a great big house at Dolphin Bay, have an art gallery at the side and Olga and Ruby and I can take these kids off your hands and love them for ever. We can be one huge family. And you can slope off back to your independent life in Sydney, being the world's best architect.'

'I…'

'I'm serious, Pierce,' she said, and she sounded serious. The laughter had gone from her voice. 'Wendy told me you wouldn't ask me to marry you because you thought I'd hate being tied to the kids. Is that true for you? For I'm making you an offer, and I mean it. You can go back to your old life and we'll live happily ever after without you.'

She took his breath away. What she was offering was so immense that he felt dizzy.

His old life back. Independence.

Wendy, Donald, Bryce, Abby, Bessy, Shanni, Ruby and Olga living in a glorious muddle of happy-ever-after in Dolphin Bay.

Without him.

The choice was a no-brainer.

The thought of being without them was suddenly so bleak he couldn't bear it.

'No.'

'No? Then the next alternative is the same thing only without me in the equation,' she said. 'If you really don't want me, then I can visit.'

'No.'

'I can't visit?'

'No, I don't not want you.'

'I'm having a little bit of trouble here,' she said.

But suddenly it was crystal clear. A man had to do what a man had to do. She'd done the proposing. She'd thrown her heart into the ring. She'd told him she loved him. The abyss she'd put before him—life without any of them—made him see what he hadn't been able to see until now.

He was deeply, madly, wildly in love with each and every one of them. Even Olga's curlers.

But most of all...

He dropped to one knee.

'Shanni.'

'Ooh,' she said.

He took her hands in his. 'Shanni, I love you.'

'Really?' She looked pleased.

'If you make any wisecracks I'm stopping.'

'I'm not making any wisecracks. Though there's a cow pat right to your left.'

'Shut up.'

'Yes, dear.'

'I love you and I want you to marry me,' he said, and suddenly the laughter was behind them. She was still smiling, but her eyes were misting with tears.

'Pierce, are you sure?'

'I've never been so certain of anything in my life. I love you so much I can't bear to think of you giving up anything. I want you to have the perfect life, and here I'm saddling you with all of us.'

'If you weren't attached you wouldn't be half as sexy.'

'Really?'

'Well, no,' she admitted. 'There's jam on your collar.'

'Shanni…'

'Yes?'

'Will you marry me?'

She gazed down at him for a long minute. She smiled and smiled and smiled.

Then she dropped to her knees to join him. She tugged him into her arms and she held him

The world shifted. For Pierce the world had been hauled out of kilter, somewhere about the time he'd been born. Ruby had tried her best to right it, but it had taken this woman, this glorious red-headed wood sprite, to finally teach him how the world should be. His Shanni. His miracle. His miracle bride.

And it seemed she was. 'Of course I'll marry you,' she whispered. 'Of course I will. Oh, my love. My Pierce. Welcome home.'

It was a honeymoon haven.

No person under the age of eighteen may visit Paradise, the brochure had said. *Visitors to this island can be assured of a tranquil, tropical idyll, without the intrusion of children and their associated noise. Pristine beaches, magnificent rainforest, luxurious chalets and most of all...privacy.*

Shanni and Pierce had been there for three days. Their honeymoon. Three days of married bliss, with not a child in sight.

'For, much as I love our kids, I'll be damned if I'm taking them on my honeymoon,' Pierce had decreed, and he'd been masterly in his ultimatum, taking charge, a man who'd had to do what a man had to do.

And by the time her parents, Ruby, Olga and Susie had had their way with their Dolphin Bay wedding—two flower girls, two page boys, six groomsmen, one gorgeous, beaming seventy-year-old matron of honour and so many friends and relations that even Shanni had felt overwhelmed—she'd meekly agreed.

They lay now in a sheltered cove, their own idyllic place. No more than six couples at a time came to Paradise and there were beaches to spare. Shanni lay in Pierce's arms. The sun was shining softly on her face. She was sated with love and with happiness…

'Anchors ahoy, look lively, avast ye swabs…'

The peace of their morning was shattered. They looked up and saw a huge inflatable dinghy being paddled their way. Two men on paddles. Four kids within.

Blake and Nik and Wendy and Bryce and Donald and Abby.

Pierce scrambled to his feet, tugging a dazed Shanni with him. They were coated in sand. They'd been tumbling in the shallows. They'd been…

Well, some things were best left unexplained. Suffice to say Shanni was blushing as Pierce tugged her down to the water's edge to meet the incoming dinghy.

'You haven't rowed all the way from the mainland, have you?' Pierce demanded as the dinghy beached and the kids tumbled out, whooping, splashing, surrounding them with laughter.

'We hired a yacht,' Nik said proudly. 'Ruby and Olga and Bessy are still on board.'

'Ruby's the captain,' Wendy said, and giggled. 'But Sam's helping.'

Sam. Another brother.

'You're not allowed here,' Pierce said, trying to sound stern, and failing.

'We know that,' Wendy said. 'We rowed into two beaches before we found you, and the people told us. But we're just checking.'

'To make sure you aren't missing us too much,' Abby explained. 'Are you?'

'Yes,' Shanni said, laughing so much she felt like crying. She swept Abby into her arms and hugged her.

'You want to come home with us?' Bryce asked.

'No,' Pierce said, and his brothers grinned.

'Hey, bro, you really telling us, your family, that you don't want us?' Nik sounded wounded.

'For two weeks I don't want you,' Pierce growled. 'Then I've got you for the rest of our lives.'

'You can have another honeymoon,' Abby said. 'When you really, really need one.'

'Are you sure you're not sick of this one?' Wendy said. 'It looks lonely to me.'

'It's not so lonely as you'd notice,' Pierce said and then, as her face fell, he grinned and lifted her with the same ease Shanni had lifted Abby. 'You're having fun on your holiday. We're having fun on ours.'

'We've got lunch,' Abby said. 'Sandwiches. Do you want to have lunch with us?'

'Yes,' Shanni said, and giggled.

'You can start your honeymoon again after lunch,' Nik said, grinning at her.

'Don't grin at my wife,' Pierce said.

'He can grin all he likes at me,' Shanni declared. 'He's family. Uncle Nik. Where are the sandwiches?'

'You'll be arrested,' Pierce said.

'Then we'll all be locked up together,' Shanni retorted, put Wendy down and grabbed Pierce's hand. 'Which is as it should be. This is perfect. Little bits of honeymoon interspersed with little bits of family.'

'Lots of family,' Pierce said.

'You love it and you know it,' she said serenely. 'Little bits of honeymoon interspersed with lots and lots of family. For the rest of our lives.'

MILLS & BOON PUBLISH EIGHT LARGE PRINT TITLES A MONTH. THESE ARE THE EIGHT TITLES FOR DECEMBER 2007.

TAKEN: THE SPANIARD'S VIRGIN
Lucy Monroe

THE PETRAKOS BRIDE
Lynne Graham

THE BRAZILIAN BOSS'S INNOCENT MISTRESS
Sarah Morgan

FOR THE SHEIKH'S PLEASURE
Annie West

THE ITALIAN'S WIFE BY SUNSET
Lucy Gordon

REUNITED: MARRIAGE IN A MILLION
Liz Fielding

HIS MIRACLE BRIDE
Marion Lennox

BREAK UP TO MAKE UP
Fiona Harper

MILLS & BOON™
Pure reading pleasure

MILLS & BOON PUBLISH EIGHT LARGE PRINT TITLES A MONTH. THESE ARE THE EIGHT TITLES FOR JANUARY 2008.

BLACKMAILED INTO THE ITALIAN'S BED
Miranda Lee

THE GREEK TYCOON'S PREGNANT WIFE
Anne Mather

INNOCENT ON HER WEDDING NIGHT
Sara Craven

THE SPANISH DUKE'S VIRGIN BRIDE
Chantelle Shaw

PROMOTED: NANNY TO WIFE
Margaret Way

NEEDED: HER MR RIGHT
Barbara Hannay

OUTBACK BOSS, CITY BRIDE
Jessica Hart

THE BRIDAL CONTRACT
Susan Fox

 MILLS & BOON®
Pure reading pleasure

1207 Rom LP